Emily Harvale lives in East Sus
You can contact her via her v
Instagram or Pinterest.

Author contacts:
www.emilyharvale.com
www.twitter.com/emilyharvale
www.facebook.com/emilyharvalewriter
www.facebook.com/emilyharvale
www.pinterest.com/emilyharvale
www.instagram.com/emilyharvale

***

Scan the code above to see all Emily's books on Amazon

Also by this author:

Highland Fling

Lizzie Marshall's Wedding

The Golf Widows' Club

Sailing Solo

Carole Singer's Christmas

Christmas Wishes – Two short stories

A Slippery Slope

The Perfect Christmas Plan – A novella

Be Mine – A novella

***

The Goldebury Bay series:

Book One – Ninety Days of Summer

Book Two – Ninety Steps to Summerhill

Book Three – Ninety Days to Christmas

***

The Hideaway Down series:

Book One – A Christmas Hideaway

Book Two – Catch A Falling Star

Catch A Falling Star

Emily Harvale

Copyright © 2016 by Emily Harvale.

The right of Emily Harvale to be identified as the Author of this Work has been asserted.
All rights reserved.
No part of this publication may be reproduced, transmitted, copied or stored in a retrieval system, in any form or by any means, without the prior written permission of the publisher and author. Nor be otherwise circulated in any form of binding or cover other than that which it is published and without a similar condition including this condition, being imposed on the subsequent purchaser.
All characters and events in this publication, other than those clearly in the public domain, are fictitious and any resemblance to real persons, living or dead, is purely coincidental.

ISBN 978-1-909917-14-9

Published by Crescent Gate Publishing

Print edition published worldwide 2016
E-edition published worldwide 2016

Editor Christina Harkness

Cover design by JR, Luke Brabants and Emily Harvale

Acknowledgements

My special thanks go to the following:

Christina Harkness for editing this novel. Christina has the patience of a saint and her input is truly appreciated.

My webmaster and friend, David Cleworth who does so much more for me than website stuff.

Luke Brabants and JR for their work on the gorgeous cover. JR is a genius in graphic design and Luke's a talented artist. Luke's website is: http://www.lukebrabants.com

My fabulous friends for their support and friendship.

All of my Twitter and Facebook friends, and fans of my Facebook author page. It's great to chat with you. You help to keep me (relatively) sane!

To the members of my new Street Team. I love that you want to help promote my books and spread the word. You're the best!

And finally, you – for buying this book. Thank You. It really means a lot to me. I hope you enjoy it.

This book is dedicated to Kitty Webb – a true friend and confidante.

Chapter One

He was in love with someone else. Laurel knew that. And because that 'someone else' was a friend of hers, he was now off limits.

That didn't mean – much to her annoyance – she wouldn't behave like a love-sick teenager whenever she saw him. Or that her heart wouldn't thump her in the chest as if to say: "He's here. Look, Laurel, it's him," every time he walked into a room, or towards her in the street or, as he had this Saturday morning and did almost every morning at seven-thirty – into her café, The Coffee Hideaway.

'Morning, Laurel,' he said, with an unmistakable trill of happiness and a smile as wide as a saucer.

'Morning.' She found it difficult to say his name these days and reminding herself that she was thirty-one, not sixteen, didn't make an iota of difference.

Stop being such a bloody drama queen, she told herself as he wound his way towards her through the crowd of empty tables.

She used to love to watch his every move. Especially on days like this when he hadn't bothered with a jacket and she could see his taut muscles beneath his black T-shirt, only partially hidden by an open, denim shirt. Surreptitiously ogling his body was a guilty pleasure and she often conjured up scenarios in her mind. Her favourite was of him silently striding towards her, leaping over the counter and pulling her to him in a passionate kiss before declaring his undying love. The sort of thing one of the heroes would do in the Gabriella Mann romance novels she'd been binge-reading since Christmas.

But there was little joy in the experience these days. Dragging her gaze from the waistband of his jeans, Laurel reminded herself yet again, there was no point in wanting someone she could never have. Ned Stelling was in love with someone else.

She turned away to prepare his usual large cappuccino before he had even ordered it.

'That's a pretty dress,' he said.

'Thanks.' Not so long ago that tiny compliment would have thrilled her. Now she knew he was merely making conversation. 'You sound happy.' She twisted the knob above the steaming wand to expel any residual droplets of water.

'I *am* happy. Ivy's coming home today, and as it's May Bank Holiday weekend, we'll get to spend three days together.'

'Oww!' The hissing steam seemed to mock her as she pulled her hand from beneath its scalding spray.

'You okay?'

Ned rushed around the counter towards her, lifting the dividing flap but Laurel held up her other hand in a stop gesture.

'I'm fine. I'm just a bit tired this morning, that's all. I wasn't paying attention.' She sucked at her stinging fingers.

He stopped, tilted his head to one side and furrowed his brows. 'Late night?'

'No.' She glanced up at him and saw the concern in his brown eyes. She wished she could say, "Yes. I spent the entire night having rampant sex with my boyfriend." But he knew she didn't have a boyfriend. That was one of the problems about living in a small village like Hideaway Down: everyone knew everything about each other.

Well, almost everything.

'Let me take a look.'

He reached out but she stepped back, clutching her wounded hand to her chest.

'You shouldn't be this side of the counter, you know. Health and Safety would string me up if they came in and saw you.' She waved a hand to shoo him away.

He stared at her for a moment before returning to the customer side, closing the flap behind him.

Laurel went to the sink which was just a few feet to her left, turned on the tap and let the cool water run over her fingers. It wasn't a serious burn but it hurt like crazy. She dabbed them dry with the corner of a red and white checked towel and continued making the coffee.

'Are you really okay, Laurel?'

She didn't look round.

'Yes. I told you. It's just a slight burn. Nothing serious. I'll live.'

A few seconds later, she banged the cardboard cup on the counter and thumped on the plastic lid.

He frowned, looking down at the cup and then up at her. 'I didn't mean your fingers. You... you don't seem yourself this morning.'

Their eyes locked and for a second, Laurel couldn't breathe.

She shook her head, waved an arm in the air and tried to sound flippant. 'No. Today I thought I'd be Perdita Baron.' She forced a smile.

'Who?'

Where on earth had that come from? Was she

completely insane? Why had she said something as stupid as that? Probably because the name had constantly popped up on her social media feeds yesterday, and today it seemed to have gone viral. She had even heard it at least five times on the radio this morning since getting up at five o'clock.

'The actress. The one who's been all over the news because of her break-up with Jamie McDay.'

Laurel pretended she knew what she was talking about and prayed he wouldn't ask for details. She didn't know any, other than what she had heard. She wasn't really into celebrities and couldn't remember the last time she'd been to the local cinema in Eastbourne. Or watched TV at home, for that matter. Running the café occupied most of her time and when she wasn't doing that, Laurel liked to get out into the great outdoors and breathe in the fresh air, not sit in her cosy one-bed flat above her business. And there was an abundance of 'the great outdoors' merely a stone's throw away – fields, woods, and lakes – the dramatic, sweeping, yet crumbling cliffs bordering the English Channel. You name it, Hideaway Down was surrounded by it.

'Er…who's Jamie McDay? Another actor?' Ned looked lost.

Laurel wasn't the only person who didn't know one celebrity from another. Sometimes it seemed to her that very few people in Hideaway Down had any interest in what was going on in the world around them. They were aware of all the current, serious issues of course, like terrorism and climate change; foreign and domestic politics; the NHS; education; and pensions. These and other such important topics were regularly debated over a pint or two in The Snowdrop Inn. Sometimes the debates became heated and one of the regulars would storm out in a huff, vowing never to return but would be back the following day chatting amiably with the very people they had rowed with. The villagers simply didn't seem to discuss less weighty issues, like films or fashion, or who was sleeping with whom in the world at large. Although they did discuss the minutiae of their own everyday lives. And everyone else's in the village. If something happened to one of the villagers, no matter how trivial, every single resident knew all the details, usually within minutes of it taking place. And they were all eager to give their opinions on the matter, whether asked for or not.

'Uh-huh,' Laurel said, recalling as much as she could of what she'd heard and reciting it parrot fashion. 'Perdita Baron is one of the biggest stars in Hollywood. She's just confirmed that her relationship with her equally sparkling co-star, Jamie McDay is over after he was, allegedly, arrested for causing a public disturbance and assault. Although why he punched Rod Finer, the president of Finer Pictures, one of Hollywood's major film studios, is still a mystery.'

'Oh, I see.' He clearly didn't but then neither did Laurel. 'You sounded like a reporter. They must be pretty famous. Should I have heard of them?'

'Not unless you're into vampires, I suppose. Perdita and Jamie rose to meteoric stardom after their comedy vampire movie: *Keep a Lid on It*, broke box office records three years ago. They'd just wrapped up filming, *Keep a Lid on It 3* when Jamie's outburst occurred. Sources say that McDay's behaviour has been of increasing concern of late and rumours are circulating that he may be axed from the hit movie franchise.'

Ned grinned and twisted round, glancing at the walls and ceiling. 'Are you reading that from an autocue or something?'

Laurel pulled a face. 'Just stating the facts as I remember them. Anyway, I must get on. Lots to do before the masses arrive for the May Day celebrations. Have a lovely day.'

As she turned away and wiped some spilt coffee from the machine's drip tray, she could feel him watching her. Or perhaps she was imagining it. Why? Why? Why couldn't she behave like a normal human being around him instead of some gibbering idiot?

'And you,' he said, after a moment. 'Say hello to Trixie for me.'

'Will do,' she replied, knowing very well she wouldn't. The last thing she needed was another lecture on love from her mother.

And Trixie French was good at giving lectures. Not just about love, either. If it were an Olympic sport, she could lecture for Great Britain and win Gold with her eyes closed.

'Tell him how you feel,' Trixie would say. 'It's obvious you're in love with him. Men are hopeless. You can't sit and wait for them to come to you. You have to go to them. They never know what's best for them. You have to tell them.'

'I'm not in love with him,' Laurel would reply for the umpteenth time. 'We're just friends. Good friends.'

'Friends, my eye! Your very first steps as a chubby toddler were in his direction, and you didn't just walk. Oh no. You dashed headlong towards him. You've been making a beeline for him ever since. Though he's clearly too daft to see it and you're too silly to do anything about it. Friends. Pah! You've got to grab the bull by the horns, my girl. But now he's with Ivy Gilroy it'll be more difficult. Never mind. What you need to do is tell him. Tell him you're the one he should be with. Don't wait until he's standing at the altar with someone else.'

'Yes, Mum. I'll get on to that right away,' Laurel would say, knowing that was something else she would never do.

Her mum had some very strange ideas as far as men – and love – were concerned. And friendship, come to that.

But Laurel had to admit that her mum was right about one thing: Laurel did feel as if she'd been walking towards Ned Stelling her entire life. She'd certainly been in love with him for most of it. Not that Ned seemed to have noticed. Or care for that matter. Her love was unrequited. Now Ned was in love with Ivy Gilroy. And Ivy was her friend.

None of that bothered Trixie. Nor did the fact that Trixie had been lifelong friends with Ivy's mum, Janet Gilroy. Trixie believed that all was fair in love and war. If you wanted something, or someone, you went all out to get them, stepping over the bodies on the way. A concept Laurel couldn't agree with, no matter how hard her mother tried to persuade her. Or how much Laurel wanted Ned.

Laurel waited a second before turning round to watch him leave. As he reached the door, she had an irrational urge to run after him. To find some excuse to make him stay longer. But she didn't. She couldn't.

Instead, she leant her elbows on the counter and propped up her chin as he swung open the bright red door. Why had she held up her hand to stop him, earlier? He might have taken her hand in his; offered to rub soothing ointment on her burn; wrapped his arms around her and…

'Sorry, Laurel. I missed that.' Ned turned in the doorway to face her, a questioning look in his dreamy eyes. 'What did you say?'

'What?' She straightened up abruptly. Had that loud sigh escaped her? It was just the sigh, wasn't it? She hadn't actually said any of that out loud… had she? 'Um.' She sighed again, this time shrugging her shoulders in a meaningful way. 'I was just saying that it looks like we'll have rain today and I was hoping for sun. I've put some washing out.'

She closed her eyes for a brief moment. She was such a dork at times. First going on about a couple of actors she hadn't even heard of until yesterday. Now, washing. And rain? No wonder Ned wasn't the least bit interested in her. Ivy Gilroy – the love of Ned's life according to the village gossips – wouldn't say stupid stuff like that, that's for sure. There wasn't a cloud in the sky and when Laurel had come downstairs to open the café at seven o'clock this morning, the sun was already peeping over Hideaway Cliff, its pale golden rays burning off any lingering morning dew from the rooftops and pavements of Hideaway Down. It was clearly going to be a gorgeous, spring day, and very warm for the last day of April. Perfect May Bank Holiday weekend weather, in fact.

Ned smiled. 'I hope it doesn't rain. Ivy's driving down this morning and even though it's the Bank Holiday weekend, I'm going to close the smithy at twelve and have a very long lunch break. I'm taking her on a picnic.'

'Really?'

Laurel was surprised by that. The May Day celebrations were one of the big events on the village calendar and lasted for three days. They began with the May Day Saturday Market – somewhat odd this time as today was the 30th of April, but as Bank Holiday Monday was early this year, there was nothing that could be done about it. The villagers certainly weren't going to change the name of the market simply because the Saturday happened to fall on the last day of April. The market attracted visitors from miles around and the Blacksmith's

Forge, along with all the other village businesses, was usually crowded with customers eager to be parted from their money. In previous years, Ned wouldn't so much as close his smithy for five minutes to have a sandwich, let alone for a couple of hours to take his girlfriend on a picnic.

Ned nodded. 'Yeah. There'll be so much going on, they can do without a blacksmith for an hour or two. I've asked Maisy to have a freshly baked French stick and a couple of her delicious cakes ready for me, and I've bought some of Ivy's favourite stinky cheese from the deli. That, a few slices of ham, some salad stuff and a bottle of wine and hey presto. A surprise picnic up at Hideaway Hole. It should be quiet up there because everyone will be at the market or in the village shops.'

'That sounds wonderful.'

It did, and Laurel could see them now, whiling away a couple of hours in a daffodil-strewn meadow beside the serene waters of the lake at Hideaway Hole, surrounded by fields of frolicking lambs. That was a picture she wanted to erase from her mind as quickly as possible. But she couldn't help wishing she could be in Ivy's shoes. And in Ned's arms.

'And romantic, I hope. I want this weekend to be special.'

Laurel's skin prickled. 'Special? Why?'

'I haven't seen Ivy for almost three weeks. She's been so busy at work due to her big promotion. The last time we spent any real time together was the four days over Easter and that was at the end of March! I haven't been able to get up to London to spend the weekend with her because I'm chasing my tail at the forge. Orders have been pouring in since Easter. We've only been able to grab a few hours on one Sunday between then and now. What with Mum being so unwell, I couldn't leave her for too long.' He shook his head.

Ned and his mother, Audrey, were very close. He wasn't a 'mummy's boy' by any stretch of the imagination, either in the looks department or in attitude, but he did do a lot for her and was always nipping round to see if she needed anything. Many a mother who attended services at St Catherine's, the village church where Audrey helped out, believed *The Good Lord* had sent Audrey such a wonderful son as Ned as a reward for her many good deeds and kindness to the community in general. Audrey believed she'd been given Ned in exchange for having such a useless husband. The only good thing Edward Stelling had done, as far as Audrey was concerned, was die, shortly after their son, Ned was born.

'How is your mum?' Laurel asked, even though she knew the answer. If someone so much as coughed, the entire village knew about it in five seconds flat. Besides which, Laurel popped in to see Audrey and take her a cup of coffee and a chocolate muffin – Audrey's favourite – from time to time. 'Mum and I called round on Monday and she seemed so much better.'

He nodded. 'She is, thank heavens. That's why I'm looking forward to this weekend so much. I can spend nearly all my time with Ivy and not be worrying about Mum.'

Audrey had been ill, on and off, since she caught flu over the New Year. She'd even had to spend a few days in hospital due to 'complications' but since Easter she'd been picking up; her breathing had returned to normal and the colour had reappeared in her sallow cheeks. She was improving on a daily basis and, it was hoped, would soon be up and about, arranging the floral displays at St

Catherine's and generally keeping the church and the vicar, Kev the Rev, in order.

Ned didn't live at his mum's but during the worst of her illness he had stayed over. Now he was back in his own spacious flat above his smithy, which was about a two-minute walk down Market Street from Laurel's café and a further five minutes from Church Cottages where Audrey Stelling lived, at number two.

Over the years, Laurel had often wondered why Ned came to The Coffee Hideaway almost every morning for his cappuccino when he could easily have made his own coffee and taken it downstairs to his blacksmith's shop, or nipped round to his mum's. Not that Laurel minded. In fact, she was very glad he did. Ned's visits had brightened her day on many a cold, grey morning. Although not as much as they once did.

'It's because he wants to see *you*,' Trixie frequently told her. 'The man's half in love with you. He just needs a little encouragement to persuade the other half. You need to tell him how you feel, my girl.'

'So you keep saying, Mum. But it's not me he's in love with. It's my coffee,' Laurel argued.

And she was clearly right. Because at Christmas, Ned had started dating Ivy Gilroy and Laurel was certain of one thing: Ned Stelling had never looked at her – or her coffee – the way he looked at Ivy.

Now Laurel almost dreaded seeing him. She still couldn't believe how much it hurt to know that she and Ned would never be anything more than friends. And she couldn't stop herself from feeling just a little bit envious every time she saw Ned wrap an arm around Ivy and pull her close.

But he was happy, and that was the important thing.

'Anyway,' Ned continued. 'I'd better get going. That

iron won't shape itself and I need to get as much done as possible before Ivy arrives.'

Ned must be crazy about Ivy. He'd been saying how busy he was and yet, because Ivy was coming home, he was not just willing but eager to shut the smithy.

'Yes. I've got lots to do today, too. Better get on.'

'Have a lovely day, Laurel.'

'Thanks. Same to you.'

'Watch it!'

A tall man with milky-white skin and eyes as dark as roasted coffee beans, glowered as Ned turned to step outside, bumping into him.

Ned gave him an apologetic smile. 'Sorry! My fault. I wasn't looking where I was going.'

'Too busy drooling over your girlfriend.'

'What?'

The man nodded towards Laurel. 'Your girlfriend. She's looking at you like a love-sick cow.'

Laurel gasped. 'No I'm not! And I don't look like a cow.'

'She's not my girlfriend.' Ned looked equally embarrassed.

The man glanced from one to the other and shrugged. 'My mistake. Are you leaving? I'm dying for a decent cup of coffee and you're standing in my way.'

Ned blinked. 'Um. Yeah. I'm leaving. Er. Best coffee in the village, here.'

'Only coffee in the village from what I can see.' The man edged his athletic-looking frame past Ned and marched towards the counter without a backward glance.

'Bye then, Laurel.' Ned waved, giving the man an odd look.

'Bye.' Laurel strained to peer around her second customer of the day.

She watched as Ned strode past her window towards his smithy. When he was out of sight, Laurel turned her attention to the stranger. He clearly hadn't been paying any attention to her or Ned. He was scrutinising the blackboard above the counter and he didn't look pleased.

Laurel studied his face for a moment. His pale skin was completely at odds with both his stature and his undeniably handsome features. He should be tanned the colour of mocha coffee with such large, dark eyes and thick hair as black and shiny as her polished granite counter. His black leather jacket only emphasised his pale complexion and the midnight-blue sweater he was wearing did him no favours. Even his jeans were dark. He looked tired, as if he hadn't had a good night's sleep for some time and the dark circles under his eyes added a haunted look. And yet there was something about him that made him seem... very appealing. Mesmerising, almost.

Laurel took a deep breath and smiled.

'Good morning. What can I get you?'

'A better menu. Are these the only coffees you serve? *Cappuccino, Latte, Mocha, Espresso* and... *Laurel's*? What the fuck is a *Laurel's*?'

So much for the appeal. Laurel grit her teeth and glowered.

'Firstly, I'd appreciate it if you didn't use that sort of language when speaking to me, thank you very much. Secondly, we don't feel the need for a long list of names for coffee in Hideaway Down. I can make you anything you want if you tell me how you like it, but I won't give it a clever name. *Laurel's* is freshly ground coffee with water or milk. Coffee is coffee.'

He raised dark brows. 'That shows how much you know. Never went to Barista School, I take it.'

'No. But I'll go there if you'll go to the school of good

manners. Do you want a coffee or not?'

He blinked and a hint of a smile curved his lips, but it didn't reach his eyes. 'So... *cappuccino, mocha* and... *Laurel's*, aren't clever names then?'

'No.'

He waited as if he expected her to continue.

'That's it? That's all you've got? Just "No"?'

'Yes. Can I get you a coffee or not?'

'I can see why this place is called The Coffee Hideaway. The coffee's in hiding. *Real* coffee shops have a wider variety.'

'And *real* men have good manners, but c'est la vie. If you don't like what's on offer, I suggest you go and find somewhere that meets with your exacting requirements.' She folded her arms across her chest.

He looked her up and down and this time his smile did reach his eyes. They twinkled with something akin to devilment.

'I didn't say I didn't like what was on offer. I said I'd like more of it.' He leant forward, placing long, slim fingers on the counter and fixing her with his gaze. 'Speciality coffees aren't just names, they're recipes. They're something to be savoured and enjoyed. They're like cocktails. I used to tend bar several years ago. If you asked me for a *screaming orgasm,* I'd know exactly how to give you one.'

Warmth crept into Laurel's cheeks. This guy was really something – and not in a good way. She smiled in what she hoped was a provocative manner and leant towards him, meeting his gaze.

'I think you meant, 'make you one'. Equal shots of vodka, Baileys, Kahlua and amaretto with milk and cream. I've had more than my fair share of *screaming orgasms*, it may surprise you to know. They're old news these days.

But now I know the perfect coffee for you.' She straightened up. 'Five shots of espresso with three floating coffee beans on top. It's one my brother makes. He's a barista in New York. It's called, '*A Broken Jaw*' and I'd be more than happy to *give* you one.'

He blinked again, knit his brows and then burst out laughing. 'Oh, I get it.'

'Yes. I expect you do. And frequently, I would imagine.'

'Okay. I apologise. Truce? I'll have a double espresso over brewed coffee... please. That's called a—'

'I know what that's called. Barista-brother in New York, remember? Take-away or drink here?'

He grinned. 'Oh, drink here. Definitely.'

Laurel turned to make it. 'You shouldn't drink that much coffee, you know. It's bad for you. That's probably why you're so grumpy and rude.'

'Er... perhaps you should mention that to your brother. I'm astonished anyone can actually drink that many shots of espresso in one cup. But more to the point, don't you work in a coffee shop? I don't think your boss would like to hear you tell customers that coffee's bad for them. Besides, I'd be in a far worse mood if I didn't have coffee. You wouldn't want to see me first thing in the morning before I've had at least one fix of caffeine. And now I'm babbling.'

She finished making his order and turned to look him in the eye.

'I wouldn't want to see you first thing in the morning before, or after, you've had caffeine. And this is *my* café so I'll tell my customers whatever I want.' She grabbed a saucer and placed it, and the cup on the counter. 'Anything else I can get you?'

His fingers brushed hers as he reached for the cup. He

must have touched her burnt skin because she felt a tingling sensation. She pulled her hand away. Only it wasn't the one she'd burnt.

'So you must be Laurel.' He took a sip of coffee and sighed before fixing her with an odd look. 'Hmm. I'll definitely ask for a *Laurel* next time. I'd like to know what that tastes like. I can already tell it'll have the perfect body. And that's important… for a coffee.'

Chapter Two

Laurel couldn't remember the last time she had been so pleased to see her mother. The stranger had unsettled her and even though she could give as good as she got, banter-wise, the look in his dark eyes made her feel uncomfortable. That remark about a *Laurel* having the perfect body had nothing to do with the strength or flavour of her coffee. He was flirting with her. But why?

Perhaps he was simply paying her back for her comments. Perhaps he was one of those men who flirted with every woman he met. Perhaps he had poor eyesight. Whatever the reason, the strange sensation she had experienced when his fingers brushed hers and again, when he had licked his lips after that ridiculous sentence, had taken her completely by surprise.

She should dismiss it. It was a throw-away line and meant nothing. Her body was a long way from being perfect, she knew that. Especially now. She wasn't particularly pretty either. She had what her mother called 'an interesting face'. Her brother, Graydon, once played dot-to-dot, using her freckles and a pen with indelible ink. That was the only occasion when Laurel could recall her mum shouting at Graydon. He was Trixie's 'golden boy' most of the time, with his father's wavy blonde hair and angelic features. Laurel got her mother's gingery-brown, straight as a poker, hair and her paternal grandmother's fair, freckled complexion. Not a wonderful combination.

And Laurel was leaning towards 'cuddly' even before she had put on almost a stone in weight since Christmas.

Thankfully, due to her height of five feet seven and the fact that the weight seemed fairly evenly distributed (although perhaps a little extra had settled on her hips and bust) she could get away with it. Just. But not for much longer if she carried on the way she was going.

Comfort eating her mother called it. Laurel didn't find anything comforting about having to breathe in every time she tried to do up her size fourteen jeans. Which was why she had taken to wearing dresses more often. The floral-patterned one she was wearing today was pretty but she wouldn't call it especially flattering. It was half-hidden beneath her bright red apron, so it wasn't the dress that had attracted the stranger's attention in any case, although Ned had remarked on it earlier.

Her mother often told her that her legs were her best feature but they were obscured from the stranger's view by the counter, so they had nothing to do with it either. In Laurel's opinion, she looked better in jeans. She didn't like the freckles on her legs. But she did like to be able to breathe and to laugh without worrying that a button might pop off her waistband and hit a customer in the eye. At least by wearing dresses, she could do that. Not that she did laugh much lately. Or perhaps it simply felt that way.

Things had changed a lot since Christmas and it wasn't just because Ned was dating Ivy. Yes, that was a big part of it but there was also the fact Laurel didn't see as much of her best friend, Holly as she used to. Holly was now with Gabriel and they were virtually inseparable.

Laurel didn't blame Holly for that. Gabriel was gorgeous, sexy and incredibly romantic; anyone would want to spend as much time as possible with him. He was also a writer, which somehow made him seem even more desirable to be with.

Then there was the fact that Holly was negotiating to

take a lease of the premises across the street from The Coffee Hideaway and turn it into a book shop. Since the start of the year, Holly had spent hours making plans, having meetings with solicitors, her bank manager, builders and suppliers. She had little time for a leisurely coffee and a long chat with Laurel.

Not that Laurel could confide her present feelings to the person she called her best friend, anyway. Holly was Ivy's twin sister. How could Laurel admit she was in love with Ned and had been for most of her life? How could she tell Holly how she felt every time she saw Ivy and Ned together?

Although Holly would understand. She'd felt that way about Paul, until she'd met Gabriel. She'd probably tell Laurel that someone new would come along and sweep her off her feet, just as Gabriel had done with Holly. Ivy, on the other hand, would tell her to go out and have some fun. There were plenty more fish in the sea, was Ivy's motto.

Perhaps that's where Laurel should focus her attention. Perhaps she needed a new man in her life, even one she wasn't particularly interested in. It might distract her from the way she felt about Ned. Although such a strategy hadn't worked so far.

Her last relationship with an estate agent from the nearby town of Eastbourne, ended a few weeks before Christmas. Five months wasn't a long time for her to be without a man, but having spent most of the last four realising she could never have the one man she really wanted, it was beginning to feel like an eternity. At least a relationship with someone else would occupy her mind... and stop her lusting after Ned Stelling.

'Was that Ned I just saw leaving?' Trixie French fixed her gaze on Laurel, completely ignoring the stranger who stepped out of her way as she barrelled towards him, and the counter.

'Yes, Mum. And before you say another word, he was telling me how excited he is because Ivy's coming home for the weekend. He's even closing the smithy for a couple of hours over lunch to spend more time with her.'

Trixie gasped. 'He's shutting the smithy? For two hours? On May Day Saturday Market, day?'

'Yes, Mum. Don't look so horrified. It's only a couple of hours and as Ned said, there's so much going on that no one's going to panic because the smithy is closed for an hour or two. The world won't come to end because the local blacksmith takes a lunch break. But I don't want to have yet another conversation – or lecture, no doubt – about Ned, thank you very much. Let's change the subject.'

'If that tongue of yours was any sharper, you'd cut yourself, my girl.' Trixie thumped her handbag on the counter and scanned the menu.

'Would you like your usual cup of tea and two slices of toast?'

'Ooh, I shouldn't. I've not long had my porridge. But go on then. You've twisted my arm. And it's going to be a busy day. Who knows when I may get another chance to eat.' Trixie grabbed her bag and turned towards the table nearest the counter. 'I bumped into Petunia on the way here and…Oh. Who are you?'

Laurel hadn't noticed that the man had taken a seat at the table which Trixie considered to be hers.

'May I ask you to move, please?' Laurel said. 'That's my mum's table.'

'There wasn't a 'reserved' card on it.'

He glanced around the room and Laurel knew what he was thinking. He and her mum were the only two customers and the other tables were all vacant.

'I know what you're going to say but please, do us all a favour and move to one of the other tables. You can have that coffee for free if you do.'

He held her gaze for a moment before getting to his feet.

'There's no need for that. I'll happily move so that your…delightful mother can sit here.' He smiled at Trixie but Laurel could see it was fake. 'Although I can't believe you're Laurel's mum. You're far too young.'

Trixie giggled like a teenager. 'Get away with you.'

Laurel noticed the rosy glow spread across her mother's cheeks as Trixie watched the man walk towards a table near the window and sit down. How long would it take before Trixie started asking questions?

'We haven't met, have we?' Trixie's tone was cooler than her complexion. 'How do you know my daughter?' She threw Laurel a questioning look. 'Don't roll your eyes at me, Laurel. I'm only asking.'

The stranger's eyes narrowed for a moment and he smiled again. 'I don't know her. I only arrived this morning. I just came in for coffee and there she was.'

Trixie looked him up and down before shrugging off her coat and handing it to Laurel to hang on the coat stand in the corner. Laurel knew her mother too well to drape the blue gabardine mac over the back of another chair.

'Oh? From where?' Trixie questioned. 'You've got a peculiar accent. Are you passing through or hoping to stay hereabouts?'

He arched his brows. 'From the US. I've been living out there for a few years so I guess I may've picked up a certain… lilt. I'm visiting a friend, so yes, I'm planning to stay. For a short while at least.'

'The US you say? I've been to America. Where were

you?'

'When you visited, you mean?'

Laurel spotted the smirk. She was surprised he had been relatively civil to her mum until now and not simply told her to "F-off", but she didn't want to tempt Fate.

'Leave the man alone, Mum. What were you saying about bumping into Petunia?'

Trixie pouted and stuck out her chin. 'I was only being polite, Laurel. It wouldn't hurt you to try that, once in a while. People like it when someone takes an interest in them.'

'Laurel was very polite to me. She made me feel… right at home.'

Trixie and Laurel stared at the stranger, but for different reasons, Laurel knew that.

'I'm glad to hear it. She's a darling girl, of course, but that tongue of hers can cut you to the quick if she's in one of her moods.'

'Mum!'

'What? I'm only saying. So, young man. Where in America have you come from?'

'Er… L.A.' He met her continuing stare. 'Hollywood, to be precise.'

'Hollywood?' Laurel and Trixie shot a look at one another.

'Are you some sort of actor?' Trixie asked. 'You don't look like an actor. You're very pale. Do you work behind the scenes?'

He shook his head. 'No. I'm an actor. And some of us are allowed to be pale. In fact, for some roles, it's almost a prerequisite.'

'Hmm. Fancy that, Laurel. A real-life actor in Hideaway Down. Well, I never.' Trixie returned her attention to the man. 'You said you're visiting a friend.

No one we know is friends with an actor and we know everyone in Hideaway Down. Are you sure you've come to the right place?'

He looked surprised. 'Yes. My friend hasn't been here long. Perhaps you don't know him yet.'

'I just told you. We know everyone in Hideaway Down. And that means everyone. If your friend lived here, we'd know him.'

'Really? Well... his name's Gabriel Hardwick and he's staying at some place called—'

'Gabriel?' Laurel was stunned. 'You're... you're friends with Gabriel?'

He gave her an odd look. 'Yes. He told me I could come and stay for a couple of days.'

'Nonsense,' Trixie said. 'We would've known if an actor was coming to stay.'

'Holly didn't mention it to me, and neither did Gabriel,' Laurel added.

'Holly? Oh yes, the girlfriend. Do visitors need written permission or something?' He shook his head. 'You know Gabriel, then? Um... he might not've been expecting me quite so soon. It was a sort of open invitation type of thing. It just happened that I found I had some free time so I thought, what the hell, booked a ticket and here I am. I meant to call him before I left but... things got a bit manic and I forgot. I'm sure he won't mind. I often used to crash at his place in Surrey at a moment's notice.'

'So... you're saying that he isn't expecting you? That he doesn't know you're here?'

'My, my,' Trixie said. 'I'm not sure Holly will be pleased. But then again... an actor... even one who doesn't look like an actor, is still quite exciting I suppose. Are you famous?'

The man finished his coffee and stood up. 'Yes.

Although infamous is probably how best to describe me at this moment in time. Actually, I've forgotten the address and my phone battery's dead. I was going to ask you if you knew where the place was. I think it's called Ivy Gill's Happy House or something equally ridiculous but if you know Gabriel, then you'll know where he's staying.'

'It's Gilroy's Happy Holiday Cottages. And it's not ridiculous.' Laurel couldn't take this in. 'Gabriel was staying in Ivy Cottage but he moved into Holly Cottage with Holly at Easter.'

'He's moved in with her? Jesus, that was quick. They only met at Christmas.'

'He had to. Ivy Cottage was booked for the entire season from Easter onwards.'

'Oh.' He grinned. 'Not true love then? Just necessity.'

'Yes. I mean, no. That didn't come out right. They're in love. Very much in love, as it happens. Aren't they, Mum? That's why he's moved in with Holly. Because he didn't want to go back to Surrey.'

'I see.'

'Don't smirk, young man. Laurel's right. Holly and Gabriel *are* in love.'

'I believe you. Although I'm not sure why you're both trying to convince me. I couldn't give a damn either way. I just need a place to crash. They can be living on cloud nine for all I care as long as there's room for me. I assume this... cottage has a spare room?'

'Oh dear. You're right, Mum. Holly won't be pleased. Ivy's home this weekend so there's no room. Although perhaps Ivy will be staying with her mum at the pub.'

'More likely she'll be staying at Ned's,' Trixie pointed out, unhelpfully.

'Yes, of course.' Laurel didn't want to think about that.

'I'm sure this is a silly question,' the man said, looking

genuinely confused. 'But I thought Ivy was a cottage. Are you saying she's a person? Why do these people have the same names as cottages? No. Forget that. It doesn't matter. I really don't care. If you'll point me in the right direction, I'm sure Gabriel will sort something out.'

Laurel nodded. He was probably right about that. 'Um… turn right when you leave here. Walk up Market Street towards St Catherine's Church. You'll see a footpath and a stile. Follow the path and you'll see the row of four cottages up on Hideaway Cliff. Just walk towards them and you'll see the names on the doors. Holly Cottage is on the end and it has a green door.'

'How very… English,' he said, with a grin. 'Thanks. That's very helpful. But I came by car.'

'From America?' Trixie squealed.

Laurel sighed. 'From the airport, Mum. He's obviously rented a car.'

'Not necessarily. So don't give me that look. Lots of actors have their own planes. He could've brought his car over on his plane. And he did say he's famous so he must be rich enough to own a plane. Although I don't think I've ever seen him in anything.' Trixie glared at him. 'I don't watch American TV shows. So I wouldn't know. I prefer the good old British soaps. And I don't go to the cinema, not with the prices they charge. Janet and I do watch the occasional DVD but I've never seen you in one of those either. What've you been in? Something with lots of sex and violence, I expect, and we don't watch those.'

Laurel stared at her mother in disbelief. Who was she trying to kid?

The man grinned. 'Yes. There's plenty of sex and violence. Lots of dead bodies, too. And blood. I suppose, as you know Gabriel, I should introduce myself. I'm Jamie. Jamie McDay.'

'Jamie… McDay!' Laurel nearly choked.

His grinned widened. 'So you have heard of me? Nothing good, I expect.'

'No,' Laurel said. 'Nothing good. And I only heard of you yesterday.'

'I bet I can guess why that was. But never mind. That's okay. I only heard of you this morning, Laurel, but I'm definitely pleased I did. Anyway… directions to these happy holiday cottage things, by car, please?'

'What happened this morning?' Trixie queried, her gaze darting from one to the other.

'Nothing happened, Mum. He simply meant he came in, ordered coffee and we… passed the time of day. That's all.'

'I wouldn't say that.' He arched his brows. 'It had the potential to be what we in the business call a 'meet cute'.

'A meat queue?' Trixie looked bewildered. 'Is that some sort of joke?'

'Not a queue. A meet *cute*. As in two people meeting for the first time, in a way that might lead to rom—'

'Jamie!' The café door burst open and Gabriel Hardwick stood on the threshold, half grinning, half astonished. Holly Gilroy peered around him, her arm linked through his. 'I saw you from across the road. What the hell are you doing here?'

'Hello, Gabriel. You made this place sound so perfect I thought I'd come and see it for myself. Is it okay if I stay a few days?'

26

Chapter Three

'Are you sure you don't mind Jamie staying with us?' Gabriel wrapped an arm around Holly and kissed her on the cheek as they sat at the table in the window of The Coffee Hideaway. 'I'll tell him he has to find somewhere else, if you'd rather.'

Holly fidgeted in her seat and glanced in the direction of the stairs leading down to the toilets in the basement, where Jamie had headed a few seconds earlier.

'It's fine. Ivy will be staying at Ned's, so we've got the spare room. Besides, where else can he go? The cottages are fully booked and the refurbishment work on the extra bedrooms at the pub still hasn't begun despite that useless builder Mum hired, assuring her that he'd "get started in two weeks", almost five weeks ago. You know the nearest hotel's in Eastbourne. We can't send him there if he's come all this way to see you… and Hideaway Down.'

Gabriel kissed her again. 'I suspect this sudden visit has more to do with him simply wanting to get out of Hollywood for a while if what I've read and heard over the last day or two is true. He clearly wants to lie low. At least until some of the heat has died down.'

Holly fiddled with a button on her linen jacket. 'How long d'you think that'll take? He said he'd only be staying for a few days. Will things have calmed down so quickly? And why didn't you tell me about any of this when you first saw it?'

Gabriel shrugged. 'I'm sorry, Holly. Jamie's always getting himself into situations like this. I didn't think much of it, to be honest. He'd usually call me if it was something serious and I hadn't heard from him since January so I assumed everything was fine. We're not exactly bosom buddies these days. We only speak every couple of months and on high days and holidays. The last time I saw him was at my grandmother's funeral, well over a year ago. I had no idea he'd just turn up here unannounced. Although knowing Jamie as I do, I suppose I should have.'

Holly looked him straight in the eye. 'You didn't even tell me he was a friend of yours. Surely having a famous film star on speed-dial is something you should mention to the girl you're now living with?'

Gabriel grinned. 'Why? Would it have made me more attractive?'

'I'm serious.'

'Yes. So I see. Honestly, darling, it didn't even occur to me. Sorry. I'm not into name-dropping, you know that, and we've never discussed things like who our favourite film star is or whether we know anyone famous.' He pulled her to him and slid a hand inside her open jacket. 'Besides, since meeting you I've had better things to think about than Jamie McDay, believe me. And far more exciting.'

'Gabriel!' Holly slapped his hand but met the loving look in his eyes.

'Seriously. Since Christmas I've had to sort out all that business with Bryony and then find a new agent for my book. The only people I was eager for you to meet were my dad, my sister and their respective families, and arranging that at Easter was top of my priorities. Other than that, you were the only person on my mind. Mentioning that one of my friends is a Hollywood film star didn't occur to me for a second. Besides, if you'd known I was a friend of Jamie's, you might have wanted to meet him. He's got a bit of a reputation with women. They seem to fall head over heels in love with him. That's a chance I couldn't take. I wanted you to fall head over heels in love with *me*.'

She knew he was joking but she reached up and, gently tugging at a stray strand of chestnut-brown hair, pulled his face towards hers.

'I *have* fallen head over heels in love with you, Gabriel Hardwick and there isn't a man on this planet I'd rather be with.'

She leant in to kiss him but he held back.

'Wait a minute. What d'you mean, "this planet"? Are you saying there could be a man somewhere else you'd rather be with?'

Holly giggled, tugged harder and kissed him firmly on the lips. 'Idiot,' she said, when she leant back.

'Get a room you two.' Laurel brought over the coffees and a slice of chocolate cake that Gabriel had ordered and smiled down at them. 'So... first a famous author arrives in Hideaway Down at Christmas. Now a famous actor. What next, I wonder?'

'The place is becoming positively cosmopolitan,' Gabriel joked. 'Although as you'd never heard of me when I arrived and clearly had no idea who Jamie was, I'm not sure either of us can call ourselves famous in Hideaway Down.'

'Let's hope the place stays exactly as it is,' Holly said. 'Do you have any other famous friends you haven't told us about?'

Gabriel shook his head. 'None. I promise. The rest are all ordinary... but special of course in their own way.'

Holly grinned. 'Of course. As special as my friends are. At least you know my friends. I want a list later. Names, occupations, that sort of thing.'

'The minute we get home, my love.' Gabriel winked mischievously.

'Hmm. Anyway. Had you heard of him, Laurel? Jamie, I mean.'

Laurel shook her head. 'Not before yesterday when his name was plastered all over social media. I didn't really read it because all that celebrity stuff doesn't interest me very much but he was on the news on the radio today, so he must be famous. And it wasn't just a quick mention either. Obviously, if I'd known he was a friend of Gabriel's and likely to drop in and criticise my menu, I would've paid more attention.'

'Did he criticise your menu?' Gabriel looked surprised.

'Tore it to shreds. So, have you seen this comedy vampire trilogy thing he's in?'

Gabriel nodded. 'The first two, yes. They're very good, to be honest. He's a brilliant actor. He's just hopeless when it comes to real life. His character, Adam, has become a cult hero. Both Jamie and his co-star, Perdita could effectively write their own cheques. At least, Jamie could have until he flattened Rod Finer. Now he'll be lucky if he gets another cheque, let alone be able to say how many zeros it should have.'

'Why did he do it?' Laurel asked. 'Hit the guy, I mean.'

'No idea. But he'll be back in a minute. Why don't you ask him?'

Laurel flushed scarlet and averted her eyes. 'No thanks. I'd better get back to Mum or you'll have her over here asking all sorts of questions. She's just talking to Janet on her mobile. So your mum will have heard all about this, Holly. See you later.'

'Oh great.' Holly took her phone from her handbag and

placed it on the table.

Gabriel grinned. 'How long will it take her once Trixie's finished?'

'It depends whether she phones Ivy first to see if I've told my darling sister before my mum.'

Gabriel glanced over his shoulder. 'Trixie's just grabbed Jamie by the arm. I almost feel sorry for the guy. He has no idea what he's let himself in for by coming here. And it looks like Trixie's ended her call.' Holly's phone rang as he finished his sentence and he turned to her and smiled. 'Now I wonder who that could be!'

Holly smiled back and answered her phone. 'Hi, Mum. How are—?'

'Hello, darling. I'm fine thanks. Well I'm not, but that's another story. If you read about a certain builder going missing, you won't have to look any further than the village pond. Not that it's deep enough to drown the guy but I'll have a good try. Anyway, that's not why I'm calling. A little bird tells me you have a visitor. An unexpected one. And famous, apparently, although I suppose that depends on how a person defines fame. I've never heard of Jamie McDay but then the last time I went to the cinema was with your father, and we all know how long it's been since that sod ran off with his little tart.'

'And if we don't, you're sure to remind us. Yes, Mum. Jamie is a friend of Gabriel's. He'll be staying with us for a few days.'

'At the cottage?'

'Er… yes. Where else could he stay?'

'Are you sure that's wise?'

'I don't follow you. Why wouldn't it be wise?'

'Well, apart from the fact that he's a Hollywood superstar – rich, famous and good-looking, he's got a very bad reputation with women. He might try something on.

Or worse still, he might lead Gabriel astray. As Gramps would say, "You don't invite a cuckoo into your nest and expect a bed of roses." You may want to rethink this.'

'What? Hmm. I think either you or Gramps are confusing your idioms.'

'We're not confused idiots, Holly! That's not nice.'

'I said idioms, Mum, not idiots. And how do you know so much about Jamie if you hadn't heard of him?'

'The internet is a mine of information. I looked him up.'

'What? Just now? When Trixie was telling you about him?'

'Who said it was Trixie? I said "a little bird" told me.'

'Yes. And that little bird is giving our guest the third degree as we speak. I'll tell you what. Gabriel and I will bring him to the pub for lunch and then you and Gramps can interrogate him to your hearts' content. Save us a table. It'll be packed because of the May Day Market.'

'Lunch! That's perfect, darling. Oh heavens. What do Hollywood stars eat?'

'The same as the rest of us lesser mortals. Your food is excellent, Mum, so don't worry about that. We'll see you at twelve. Got to go. Bye-ee.'

'So we're having lunch at the pub,' Gabriel said, a huge grin plastered across his face. 'That'll be an entertaining experience for Jamie's first day here. I think I'd better rescue him from Trixie and, if it's okay with you, I'll take him back to the cottage. He won't have got much sleep on the flight coming over and he'll need a couple of hours of peace and quiet before he steps over the threshold of The Snowdrop Inn.'

Chapter Four

'So where is he?' Ivy Gilroy asked her sister as she shoved open the dirt-encrusted, forest green double doors of the empty shop.

Holly was balancing on the bottom rung of a stepladder, wiping several months' worth of dust and cobwebs from row upon row of wooden shelves. They lined every wall, apart from the front which, in addition to the double doors, had two large and equally filthy, square bay windows. The panes were so covered in grime that the morning sun was struggling to penetrate. One single beam had managed to find a chink but as it held a stream of dust in its slant of gold, it served only to highlight the dingy, dirty interior.

Ivy coughed as Holly stepped down from the ladder and turned to face her.

'And good morning to you too!' Holly rested her hands on her hips, a grubby grey cloth hanging from a blackened, pink rubber glove. With her other forearm, she brushed back a thick strand of auburn hair that had tumbled loose from a brightly patterned headscarf.

Ivy coughed again. 'What? Oh yeah. Morning. Bloody hell, Holly. How can you breathe in here?' Turning towards one of the wide, window display units, she grabbed a handful of junk mail from a pile and shoved a folded wad beneath each of the doors to let in some air. 'How come you're here anyway? I was really surprised when I got your message. I thought you weren't getting the keys 'til next week.'

'We weren't. But Gabriel's solicitor pulled some strings and the agents let us in a few days early. Mind you, we had to leave our kidneys and a lung as a deposit.'

'I've told you a billion-trillion times, Holly Gilroy. Don't exaggerate.' Ivy stood upright and burst out laughing. 'Sorry, but you look like the epitome of a char lady in a TV sitcom. Where's Gabriel? You're not going to let him see you looking like this, are you? He may be head over heels in love with you but believe me, this vision of loveliness will make him run straight back to his own house in Surrey.'

Holly tutted. 'For your information, he's just nipped over to Laurel's to get us some coffee. And he looks just as bad as I do.'

Ivy clasped a hand to her chest and gasped. 'This I've got to see. Gabriel in pink rubber gloves and a headscarf!'

Holly threw the filthy cloth at her but Ivy ducked out of the way in time and it landed with an explosion of dust in the doorway.

'Don't be a pain in the arse,' Holly said, grinning. The next second, looking serious. 'What's the time?'

'Don't panic. It's only nine-forty-five. I'm much earlier than expected. Mum rang me at the crack of dawn to tell me about Jamie McDay, so naturally I changed all my plans and bombed down the motorway as fast as I could.'

'Mum must've called you after she'd spoken to me and that was around eight – which is hardly the crack of dawn. Gabriel and I were having coffee in Laurel's at ten to.'

'What d'you want, a medal? When you don't get to bed before three, anything earlier than noon is the crack of dawn in my book.'

'I tried to call you myself several times but it just went to voicemail. You must have broken every speed limit to get here at this time.'

'I did. And I tried you several times, too. But who cares about that? I've been going crazy with questions.'

'I've left my handbag and my phone over at Laurel's. I didn't want to get either of them covered in dust.'

'Holly! I don't care. What have you done with Jamie McDay?'

Holly tutted. 'Okay. Okay. He's fast asleep in the spare room at Holly Cottage, as far as I know.'

'You mean... he's sleeping in my bed? Oh wow! I'm suddenly feeling rather tired. I'd better go and join him.'

'Er... Firstly, it's not your bed. It's my spare room. And secondly, does the name Ned Stelling mean anything to you? You can meet Jamie at lunchtime. We're going to the pub. Mum's saving us a table.'

'It's a date. Oh, my God! I'm going on a date with Jamie McDay.'

'No, Ivy. You're not. Now make yourself useful and give me a hand.'

'You're joking, right? Do I look dressed to do cleaning? No. I don't.'

'Hello Ivy.' Gabriel stood in the open doorway. 'You're early. Have you come to help?'

'Ah, Gabriel. There you are. And looking as angelic as usual.' Ivy kissed him on the cheek. 'I was just saying how delightful my sister looks. That outfit's rather fetching, don't you think?'

Gabriel grinned. 'I think Holly looks very sexy.'

Ivy tutted. 'That's love for you. You'd think she looked sexy in a rag. Oh wait. She's wearing a rag. Anyway, I'm told my heart-throb, Jamie McDay is sleeping in my bed. Does he know where everything is? I'd be happy to offer my services.'

Gabriel tutted. 'Don't let Ned hear you say that. I think Jamie's fine. I got him settled in and pointed him in the direction of the shower. I even explained how the Rayburn worked. Just in case. But he said that all he wanted to do was sleep.'

'I bet he got a shock when he saw that bedroom. Especially after what he's used to.' 'What's wrong with it?' Holly looked peeved.

'Nothing,' Ivy replied. 'If you're into pink and white rosebuds on the bedding, walls and curtains. Which, come to think of it, I'm sure a Hollywood superstar slash vampire, is.'

'He should think himself lucky he's got a bed to sleep in at all, after turning up unannounced.'

Gabriel grinned. 'Yeah. I don't think it's ever a problem for him to find a bed, though.'

'He can share my bed any time,' Ivy said. 'What? Don't glare at me like that, Holly. You've seen the guy. Tell me you wouldn't say the same.'

'Of course I wouldn't and I sincerely hope you're joking.'

Ivy winked at her sister before grinning at Gabriel. 'I don't suppose one of those coffees is for me, is it?'

'Nope. But I'll go and get you one if you like.'

'No. Don't worry. You and Mrs Mop stay here and get this place spic and span. I'll go over to Laurel's and find out all the gossip. I haven't seen her for weeks.'

'Are you really not going to lend a hand?' Holly asked.

'Don't look so surprised. You know I hate cleaning at the best of times. Oh, I'm joking. I do want a coffee though. And to say hello to Laurel. Then I've got to go and see Ned and let him know I've arrived safely. I called him from the motorway to tell him I'd be here much earlier than planned and I promised I'd drop in the minute I arrived. But I need to delay it for a while. If he sees me here this early, he'll start lecturing me on my driving –

and *that,* I can do without.'

'You need a lecture. One of these days you'll kill yourself. Or somebody else.'

'Yeah, yeah.'

'Holly's right. I fear for my life every time I get in a car with you at the wheel. And Ned's concerned about you because he's in love with you. You can't blame the guy for that.'

Ivy sighed. 'I suppose not. Oh bugger! I've just remembered, Ned said he's made special plans for lunch. Damn. I'll have to see if I can get him to change them. I want to join you and gorgeous Jamie in the pub. Hmm. Now what can I do to persuade him?' She laughed and waved as she turned to leave. 'See you later.'

'We might not be here when you get back,' Holly said. 'We won't be staying that long.'

Ivy glanced back. 'Oh Holly. You've become such an optimist since you and Gabriel fell in love. Look at this place. You'll be here for days and days.'

'No, we won't. We don't want to be here when the village gets really busy. The crowds will start descending for the May Day Market pretty soon. That's today, you know. So we'll be leaving here in an hour or so at the very latest.'

'Oh yeah, right. Okay. See ya. Missing you already. Can't wait to meet Jamie.'

Ivy brushed herself down as she left the shop. She'd only stood in the doorway for a few minutes but she felt as if she'd been caught in a dust storm. Even the dirt was trying to escape. Would Holly really be able to turn that dark and dingy hovel into a thriving bookshop in a matter of a few weeks? It had taken months to get to this stage and although Holly was adamant that The Book Orchard would be open before the summer, Ivy wasn't convinced.

She'd come back later and lend a hand, but for now, she needed coffee, a gossip, and to go and see Ned.

Ivy glanced up and down Market Street. The first visitors had started to arrive already even though the market didn't officially open for another fifteen minutes. Ivy may no longer live in the village but she knew all those who did and could immediately tell a stranger from a resident. There would be plenty of strangers in the village this weekend and that would be good for all the shop owners as well as the market stallholders. Hideaway Down really went to town for the May Day celebrations and there were events on each of the three days. Ivy always loved being part of it but she'd half forgotten today was a special market. How could it have slipped her mind?

The truth was, she hadn't had much time to think about Hideaway Down – or anything other than her job – since her big promotion. Being the executive assistant to the head of one of the biggest labels in the music industry meant working virtually 24/7.

She was at her boss's beck and call every minute of the day – although her boss was lovely, so she didn't mind. He often joked that she knew more about him than his wife did, which wasn't far from the truth. Ivy organised almost every detail of his life.

And it wasn't simply his life she managed. She had many other admin duties, like making sure her team had booked recording studios for the right people at the right times and then ensuring the artistes turned up when and where they were supposed to. Or getting contracts out and returned. Or providing coffee and painkillers for hungover divas. Her job also involved attending gigs and meetings, parties and dinners, launches and lunches. You name it, Ivy did it, or at the very least, was responsible for ensuring it got done.

Not that she was complaining. Ivy loved her job more than anything in the world. Well, not quite anything. She loved her sister, Mum and Gramps in equal measure. And Ned, of course. Which still surprised her. If she had been told, just six months ago, that she would be in love with Ned Stelling, she would have laughed at the suggestion. Life was very strange sometimes. But as her mum always said: "Anything can happen in Hideaway Down."

A troupe of Morris dancers, dressed from head to toe in white, save for the brightly coloured ribbons hanging from their waistbands, pranced towards her, waving equally brightly patterned hankies, scarves, flags and sprigs of green leaves. She grinned as she recognised The Hideaway Hoppers led by Bartram Battersfold, the village butcher, and Jarvis Pope, head of the Hideaway Cliff Preservation Trust and former head master at her old junior school.

'Good morning, Ivy!' Bartram's voice was as big as his belly, and both seemed to have increased, since he and the love of his life, Petunia Welsley, declared their mutual passion for each other at the Best Mince Pie competition during Christmas week last year.

'Morning, Bartram. Happy May Day weekend. You're looking particularly fetching today. And you, too, Jarvis. Off to the official opening of the May Day Market, are we?'

'We are indeed,' Jarvis said. 'You're coming to the crowning of the May Queen this afternoon, of course?'

It wasn't really a question, more of a statement and Ivy was tempted to say she wouldn't, just to see Jarvis's reaction but instead she nodded.

'Yes. I'll be there. Along with the rest of the Gilroys, as always.'

'Excellent. See you later then. We're expecting a larger turnout than ever this year.'

Bartram beamed at her. 'I still say you were the prettiest May Queen, Hideaway Down ever had. This year's Queen's got a ring through her nose! Can you believe it? A ring! I can't understand why so many people voted for her. What is the world coming to? I was only saying to my darling Petunia the other day that they don't make girls like they used to.'

Ivy tried not to burst out laughing. 'I'm sure she'll look lovely, Bartram, in spite of the ring. Perhaps you could suggest she tie a brightly coloured ribbon to it. Or perhaps a sprig of greenery.'

Bartram looked confused. 'Oh, I'm not sure about that. That would only draw attention to it, wouldn't it?'

'She was teasing, Bartram.'

Jarvis scowled at her, just like he used to when she had done something naughty at school and been dragged off to his office for a reprimand. Which happened quite a lot. She was seven-years-old again in a split second.

'Yes. Sorry, I was.'

'You girls. Honestly.' Bartram shook his head but smiled. Then, with a wave of one of the brightly coloured hankies held in his sausage-like fingers, he and the others skipped off down Market Street towards Market Field.

Ivy grinned as she watched them go, although there was a very good chance that Bartram would have a heart attack if he carried on like that. He was over fifty and fitness clearly wasn't a word he understood the meaning of, whereas Jarvis… well, that man would make a drill-sergeant weep tears of joy. She couldn't quite fathom why grown men wanted to dance around looking as if they'd robbed a haberdashers, but it takes all sorts to make a world. At least the visitors seemed to enjoy it. Almost as much as The Hideaway Hoppers.

And the visitors would just love the market. Ivy had driven past Market Field earlier and there appeared to be even more stalls than usual this year. Jarvis was right, the village would be bursting at the seams. What a shame The Book Orchard couldn't have been open in time for this weekend. Holly was missing out on potentially huge sales. But nothing could be done about that and it was probably just as well, what with Jamie McDay turning up on her doorstep.

Ivy smiled. What would he make of this weekend? A Hollywood superstar watching Morris dancers and people dressed up as trees and witches and suchlike. Hmm. Not what he was used to. Well, perhaps the witches' part wasn't too far removed from his day job. If he still had a job, that is.

As Ivy crossed the road, one of her favourite songs popped into her head and she smiled. It was rather appropriate, given the circumstances. Jamie McDay was a 'Falling Star' – or fallen to be more precise if the things she'd read and heard were true. And she'd definitely like to put him in her pocket. Or rather – get him into her bed.

Chapter Five

Laurel was wiping a damp cloth over one of the few vacant tables in The Coffee Hideaway when she glanced up and saw Ivy open the door.

'Ivy! Hi. How're you?'

'Hello, Laurel. I'm dying for a cup of your fabulous coffee… and an oxygen tank if you have one. I've just been in Holly's place and I'm struggling to breathe.'

Laurel grinned. 'Yes. She told me this morning that she was getting the keys early. She was so excited. Is it really that bad? I'm hoping to nip over and take a look later.'

'I'd wait until they've cleaned the place up if I were you.' Ivy followed Laurel towards the counter. 'Have you heard the exciting news?'

Laurel spun round. 'What news?'

Ivy laughed. 'There's no need to look so worried, Laurel. It's good news. Jamie McDay's in town!'

'Oh that.'

'Er… is that all you have to say? "Oh that!" Jamie McDay, Laurel – the film star! The most gorgeous man on this earth has come to Hideaway Down and not only that, he's a friend of Gabriel's. I could kill Gabriel for keeping that a secret. Anyway, I can't wait to meet him. Any chance you could close for lunch? We're all meeting in the pub.'

Laurel walked around the counter and slid the cloth into a small bowl of bleach on the shelf below. Ivy stopped, adjusted one of the two high stools at the front and sat down, leaning her elbows on the spotless black surface.

'The pub? But you're going... I mean. Ned mentioned you were coming home. He said he was taking you out for lunch... or something.' Laurel turned to the coffee machines. Ned had said it was going to be a surprise. Had she ruined it?

'Did he? Yeah. He mentioned that to me when I spoke to him earlier. I'm hoping I can persuade him to go to the pub instead. Okay. As you don't have an oxygen tank, I'd better have a caramel iced doughnut instead. Sugar's as good as oxygen, right? Aren't you even a tiny bit excited about Jamie McDay, Laurel?'

Laurel placed a large cup of Ivy's favourite cappuccino on the counter and grabbed the metal tongs to take a doughnut from the cake display case. She put it on a plate and handed it to Ivy.

'I can honestly say, I'd be more excited to watch paint dry at Holly's new bookshop. I've already met the man and once was more than enough, thanks very much.'

Ivy frowned. 'You're joking, right? When did you meet him? Oh, I suppose he was in here this morning with Holly and Gabriel. Weren't you even just a teensy-weensy bit in awe?' Ivy took a bite of the doughnut and sighed as if she hadn't eaten for days.

'No. I had no idea who he was when he first came in and he was bloody rude. I know he's supposed to be a heart-throb and all that but I just don't see it. He's good-looking, I suppose but nothing special and he's deathly pale. What that man needs is a few long walks over Hideaway Cliff to get some sun on his bones. He also needs to realise that he's not in Hollywood now.'

Ivy sniggered. 'I don't think he'll be in any doubt about not being in Hollywood but he may wonder if he's arrived in Lunatic Land when he sees The Hideaway Hoppers. I've just bumped into Bartram and his band of merry men heading down to woo the crowds in Market Field. Ooh. Who's the May Queen this year? Bartram mentioned she has a ring through her nose. That's rather hip for a resident of Hideaway Down. I meant to ask him, but I had Jamie McDay on my mind. What? Why does everyone give me that look when I mention Jamie's name?'

'Perhaps they're wondering why you're not mentioning someone else's name.'

Ivy winked and grinned broadly. 'Ned, you mean? Ned's great. But he's not Jamie McDay, is he?' She took another bite and closed her eyes, sighing again.

Laurel waited for a second until Ivy reopened them. 'No, Ivy. Ned is definitely *not* Jamie McDay. And you should thank your lucky stars for that.'

'Yeah, I know I should. And I do. I really do. But I've had a huge crush on Jamie ever since I saw him in that coffee commercial about four years ago and... well, now the man's here, I've gone all star-struck. I'm dying to meet him, that's all. There's nothing wrong with that, is there? This doughnut is heavenly, by the way.' Ivy popped the last bite in her mouth and grinned as she finished it.

'No. There's nothing wrong with that. As long as that's all you're dying to do.'

Ivy gave a burst of laughter. 'Laurel French! What *do* you mean?'

Laurel smirked, removed Ivy's empty plate and slid it into a large bowl beneath the counter in which there were a few other items of crockery and cutlery waiting to be put in the dishwasher.

'You know very well what I mean. But let's change the subject. Bethany Morrison is the May Queen and yes, she does have a ring through her nose. And several piercings in her left ear, I think. She's only recently turned Goth and she had them done at Easter. Bartram may not have spotted the ear piercings… yet.'

'Bethany! Wow. Let's hope she wears her hair down then and not up in a bun or something. At least she's gorgeous.' Ivy took several gulps of coffee and a second or two later, when her cup was empty, beamed at Laurel. 'I'd better go and tell Ned I'm here before someone else does.' She placed the exact money for her coffee and doughnut on the counter and popped a fifty pence piece in the tip jar, beside the cake display as she slid from the stool.

Laurel tutted. 'Ivy! You don't have to do that. Thanks very much though.'

Ivy grinned. 'What? Leave a tip? Or see Ned?' She winked. 'Have a great morning. And don't forget. Lunch in the pub with gorgeous Jamie. Twelve on the dot. Missing you already.' She waved and made her way towards the door.

'See you. Have fun.'

Laurel watched Ivy go and smiled. She waved as Ivy passed the window, pulling a face through the glass. Sometimes that woman behaved like a five-year-old instead of the thirty-one-year-old she was but she was always fun to have around, that was for sure. The life and soul of the party.

It was amazing how Ivy and Holly could be twins and yet be so different. Perhaps that was partly because they weren't identical twins. But did looks govern personalities in such cases? Holly was the more serious of the two; Ivy the more ambitious, although Holly now had the bookshop, so she definitely had aspirations of her own.

Holly loved the peace and tranquillity of Hideaway Down and never wanted to live anywhere else. An annual holiday to foreign climes was enough for her. Ivy, on the other hand, loved the bright lights of London and wanted to see as many far-flung places as she could. She'd been planning a trip to Borneo before she'd started dating Ned. Had she put that on hold? Laurel couldn't see Ned particularly wanting to go to Borneo.

'May I have four pots of tea, please?'

Laurel had been in a world of her own and hadn't even heard the latest customers come in.

'Yes, of course. Hello. Would you like anything else, or just the tea? The May Day cupcakes are delicious. They're from Maisy Miller's bakery just a few doors away and freshly made this morning. The green leaves on top are edible, as are the tiny flowers.'

The woman glanced over her shoulder towards a table where her three companions sat. 'Cupcakes anyone? They've got edible flower things. They do look lovely. I'm having one.'

'Yes please,' one of the women replied and the rest nodded in unison.

The customer at the counter grinned. 'Looks like four cupcakes then.'

Laurel smiled. 'Take a seat and I'll bring them over with your tea. Are you here for the market?'

'Yes. We come every year. And to the Easter one and the Summer Fete and the Autumn Harvest Festival one. My favourite is the Christmas one though. Especially last year's. The fact it snowed made it even more magical, didn't it? Do you live here?'

'Yes. This is my café and I live upstairs.'

The woman placed a hand on her heart. 'Ooh. You're so lucky to live in a place like this. We come from Eastbourne. Don't get me wrong, Eastbourne's lovely but Hideaway Down, well, it's like stepping back in time. It's so quaint and everyone's so friendly. And that blacksmith.' She winked. 'Shauna, my friend with the blonde hair...' She pointed towards the table at a blonde with spiky hair. '...Well, every time we come she buys something from his smithy. There's more ironwork in her house and garden now than there is in his shop.'

Laurel glanced over at Shauna. The woman clearly saw herself as a cougar. She must have been fifty, at least, but she was pretty stunning. In more ways than one. The sparkly, white top she was wearing clung to every toned inch of her torso but how she kept her head so upright with those huge, heavy earrings dangling the full length of her swanlike neck, was a mystery.

'Oops,' added the woman at the counter. 'He's not your boyfriend or anything, is he?'

'What? Oh no. No. He's just a friend. Um. He does have a girlfriend though. And... he's crazy about her, unfortunately.'

'Don't you worry about that, love. Shauna's not one to let a little detail like a girlfriend get in her way. I keep telling her the guy's not interested but she keeps coming back in case he's changed his mind. So, have you got a man in your life?'

'No. Hideaway Down may be one of the prettiest villages in East Sussex but it's not exactly teeming with available men of my age. Or available men of any age come to that. Most of them are married. In fact, at this moment in time, Ned... oh, that's the blacksmith's name... Ned and one other man called Gabriel are the only ones in their thirties, and both of them are taken. The vicar's single. But he's around forty, I think.'

The woman giggled. 'Kev the Rev! Yes. We've met him several times. He's so funny. And not at all vicarly – if that's a word. He's not bad looking. Nothing on the blacksmith though and this Gabriel... Ooh! Was he the one causing all the drama around Christmas? He's an author, isn't he?'

Oh dear. Why on earth had she mentioned Gabriel? Laurel coughed and finished making the tea, quickly placing the pots, cups, saucers and milk jug on a tray.

'Here we are. I'll bring it over and then I'll get your cupcakes.'

'I can take that.' The woman reached out and took the tray, glancing over her shoulder as she did so. 'Shauna! Get your bum off that chair and come and get our cupcakes, will you? You could do with the exercise.'

Hoots of laughter boomed out from the friends. As Shauna was clearly a size eight or less, apart from her bust, which looked about two sizes larger, it was obviously a joke all four friends found amusing.

Laurel unwittingly let out a long sigh. What she wouldn't give to have a body like that. Maybe then, Ned would leap over the counter and sweep her into his arms.

Then again, now he was with Ivy, probably not.

Chapter Six

Ned sensed someone enter through the open stable door of his smithy. Was it Ivy? Had she come at last?

He glanced up from the red-hot piece of iron he was working on which was balanced on his anvil and held in position by a pair of heavy tongs. It *was* Ivy. He threw her a quick smile. 'You're here then.' He brought his hammer down on the workpiece with considerable feeling and the resounding clang – as if he had struck the side of a massive church bell – echoed around him.

Ivy stopped in her tracks. He could see her surprise from the corner of his eye.

Damn. Why had he said it like that when what he really wanted to do was run to her and sweep her up in his arms, not scold her like a naughty child? So she'd gone to see her sister before she'd come to see him, so what? And okay, she'd gone to see Laurel and get a cup of coffee and, knowing Ivy, a doughnut; that didn't mean anything. Just because he was third on her list. Or had she been to see her mum and Gramps too?

'Is this a bad time? Shall I go away and come back later?'

'No!' He nearly dropped the hammer on his foot. That would be a great start to the weekend, wouldn't it? A broken bone. Mind you, his metal-capped boots would bear most of the brunt. 'Sorry.' He tossed the hammer onto a nearby workbench and with his tongs, carefully placed the workpiece into a cast-iron vat of water. It sizzled and hissed but when it was safely positioned, he wiped his grimy hands with a cloth and turned to Ivy, catching his breath as he did so.

God, she looked good with her long hair tumbling over the shoulders of her suede jacket and almost reaching the waistband of her fitted jeans.

'I thought you'd be pleased to see me.'

She also looked irritated.

'I am! I'm just a little disappointed you didn't come here first. I'm being an idiot, I know. Come over here and I'll show you how pleased I am.'

He held out his arms but Ivy stood her ground. She tipped her head to one side and he felt a rush of heat as she smiled at him.

'Why don't you come over here?' She dragged a finger along the length of a shelf as she slowly edged her way towards one side of the smithy, maintaining the distance between them.

Ned watched her, passion building inside him. If she carried on like that, he'd have to throw *himself* in that vat of cold water. Or go and take a cold shower. Oh God. Why did he have to think of the shower? The last time he'd had sex with Ivy was in his shower. He swallowed the thump in his throat.

'Is this a Mexican stand-off?' He forced a grin. 'Why don't we meet halfway?' He took a step forward and hoped she'd do the same. He really *was* behaving like a sulky teenager. Why couldn't he simply swallow his pride and go and grab her? That's what he wanted to do. Well, that and a lot, lot more. But sex would have to wait. He couldn't close the smithy until twelve. Not even for Ivy.

'How did you know I went somewhere else before coming here?'

She threw him a look so inviting that he shivered. He actually shivered. It still amazed him how crazy Ivy

Gilroy made him feel. Right down to his bones. He ached for her.

Take a deep breath, he told himself.

'Meg Stanbridge saw you come out of Holly's shop and go into Laurel's. I thought she was imagining it. Firstly, because I didn't know Holly had managed to get the keys early and secondly, because you'd have to have driven like the devil to get here so quickly. And we both know how much it worries me when you drive so fast, don't we?'

Ivy stopped in her tracks and frowned. 'We certainly do.'

Damn. Now she was even more annoyed. Just go to her, man, he urged himself. But he couldn't for some bizarre reason.

'One day, you'll kill yourself. Or someone else.'

'Yes. So people keep telling me. But I've been driving since I was seventeen and so far I haven't had so much as a scratched bumper.'

'That doesn't mean it won't happen. In fact with that attitude, it's even more likely to. But I won't give you another lecture on that. You know my opinion.' What was wrong with him? Sulking and lecturing. Some boyfriend he was. He stepped forward. 'Ivy, it's just—'

'Have you heard that Jamie McDay's in town?'

Her words and the expression on her face made him stop. 'Who?'

'Jamie McDay. He's a friend of Gabriel's apparently and he'll be staying at Holly's for a few days.'

'Jamie McDay? Jamie...' He'd heard that name; but where? 'Isn't that the guy Laurel told me about this morning? I mean... Laurel mentioned that name when I was getting coffee. He's here? The same guy? But he... How? I thought Laurel said he was a Hollywood film star.

I don't understand.'

Ivy picked up a door knocker forged into the shape of a Koi carp and Ned watched as she turned it over in her hands, stroking the scales he'd carved down the length of its body. God. What wouldn't he give to stroke the length of Ivy's body right now!

'He's a Hollywood superstar. And he's drop-dead gorgeous. I've had a massive crush on him for... oh, forever. And now he's here. And he's staying with *my* sister.' She returned the door knocker to its place on the shelf and beamed at him. 'And I'm having lunch with him today in the pub.'

'You're... you're what?'

'I'm having lunch with Jamie McDay. Today. In The Snowdrop Inn. Oh, don't glare at me like that! Not just me. We're all going. I was hoping you'd come too but you seem to be in a very strange mood so perhaps you'd better not.'

'Ivy! I told you I'd arranged something special for lunch. Just you and me.'

Now she came to him. 'Oh, I know you did. Please don't look so hurt. But you can cancel it, can't you? I mean... this is Jamie McDay, Ned. Jamie McDay! I'm only here for the weekend and I can't miss the chance to see him. To have lunch with him. You don't really mind, do you? You and I can have lunch any time. Jamie will probably only be here for a short while and then he'll go back to Hollywood and I'll never get the chance to see him again. Ever.' She traced a finger down his neck and under the V of his T-shirt which was hidden beneath his leather apron. 'Please, Ned. Please say you don't mind. I'll make it up to you. I promise.'

Ned looked down into her eyes. Eyes as green as the meadow where he'd been hoping to lie with her this lunchtime. Eyes as green as the precious jewel she was.

He wrapped his arms around her and pulled her close. 'I do mind, Ivy. I mind very much. But fine. We can go and have lunch with this Jamie McDay guy, if that's what you want.' He leant in to kiss her.

'We? You mean you'll come too?'

He pulled back. 'Don't you want me to?'

'Yes! Yes, of course I do. It's just that I know you're not really into this celebrity stuff. Whenever I tell you about someone famous I've met through my job, you just say: "Huh? Who?" Well, most of the time anyway. You do know some of the bands we represent, so I suppose that's something but other celebrities... well... you're as bad as Laurel on that score.'

'It's all a load of crap, this celebrity business. So they've made a film? So what? Or starred in some TV show. Now a brain surgeon, that's different. Someone who saves lives deserves to be held in awe but actors and stuff. They're ten a penny. Now come here, gorgeous.' He longed to kiss her.

Ivy placed her palms on his chest to hold him off. 'Oh really? So why do you want to meet Jamie McDay then?'

Ned took her hands in his and gently eased them behind her back, pulling her body closer to his in the process.

'I don't. What I want is to spend more time with you, Ivy Gilroy and if that means spending an hour with some actor, then so be it.'

Ivy giggled. 'Not because you're worried I might run off with him? He is gorgeous, after all. And famous.' She grinned up at him.

'Yeah. That too. Now shut up and let me kiss you. I've been dying to since the minute Meg Stanbridge told me you'd arrived.'

'Really? Hmm. You've got a funny way of showing it, Ned Stelling. I've been here for at least five minutes and all you've done so far is—'

Chapter Seven

Ivy sang the words to *Love Me Like You Do* as she left Ned's and headed up Market Street. It was one of her favourite Ellie Goulding tracks and one that in many ways seemed oddly appropriate in the present circumstances.

Ned's kiss had blown her socks off but when she'd suggested they go upstairs for five minutes he'd been his usual, serious self. God, sometimes she wanted that man so much it almost frightened her, especially when he held back as he had today even though it was obvious he wanted her as much as she wanted him. And sometimes he irritated her and made her wonder how and why they'd got together in the first place.

'I can't, Ivy,' he'd said. 'Not if I'm closing for lunch as well. It's the May Day Market today and you know the whole village will be teeming with tourists.'

'Close for… a long coffee break now then, and forget lunch. After all, wouldn't you rather spend fifteen minutes having sex with me than an hour having lunch with Jamie McDay?'

'I'd rather spend an hour making love with you than a quick fifteen-minute tumble. Why don't you meet this Jamie guy for coffee and spend the entire lunchtime with me, as we'd originally planned?'

He'd kissed her again and she'd seriously considered his proposal. She wanted his hands on her body so much and it was only being back in his arms that made her realise how badly she'd missed him. How much she wanted him.

And then he'd gone and ruined it all.

'After all, he'll be headed back to the bright lights of Hollywood in a few days. I'll still be your boyfriend, right here in Hideaway Down.'

The man should learn to quit while he was ahead.

'Precisely! That's my point, Ned. You and I can have sex anytime. Well, when you're prepared to close your smithy, we can, but Jamie won't be here forever and I'm only home this weekend. He'll be gone the next time I'm down, whereas you'll always be here.'

And that *was* the point. Having lunch with Jamie McDay was a once-in-a-lifetime opportunity. Having sex with Ned was something she would be doing for the rest of her life. Apart from during working hours, apparently.

When they'd first got together at Christmas, he'd been willing – no, eager – to close the smithy for an hour or two, and he'd been equally as busy then. What was so different now? It was simply another market day. Okay, not just any market day; it was the special May Day Market but even so. And he'd been perfectly willing to close for lunch, so why not a long coffee break? If the roles had been reversed, she'd have closed up.

Or would she?

Since her promotion she'd hardly seen Ned because she'd been so busy at work. That was different though. She lived and worked in London. Ned lived over sixty miles away in Hideaway Down. She couldn't simply pop out of the office for a quick, fifteen-minute sex break. Which she would have happily done if Ned was local to her office.

Oh, what was the point in thinking about it? It was what it was.

And it was getting busy in the village now. That was the third time she'd had to step off the pavement to avoid the crowd heading in her direction. Well, in the direction of Market Field, and she was in the way. Anyone would think some people had never been to a market before. They were almost salivating as they jostled past her.

She finally reached Holly's shop but it was empty in more ways than one. There was no sign of Holly or Gabriel. Wow. Holly had really meant it. They didn't stay long.

Ivy peered through the still grimy windows and shook her head. Apart from the step ladder leaning up against one of the walls of shelves, and the odd discarded cloth or two hanging over it, the place didn't look any different from the way it had when Ivy was last standing here, at Easter. It would definitely take a lot of work to transform it from the drab, dirty shell it was into the warm and welcoming shop Holly had described. Holly and Gabriel clearly needed help.

'Hello, Ivy. I heard you were back for the weekend. How are you?'

Ivy still found it amusing that the relatively new vicar of St Catherine's wore T-shirts emblazoned with the words: Kev the Rev, on the front. He had them in a variety of colours and on special religious days, like Christmas and Easter, they even matched the colour of the stole he hung around his shoulders, like a scarf, over his vestments. But as the May Day celebrations originated from a pagan festival, not a religious one, today's T-shirt was dark green with the words in bright yellow.

'Morning, vicar. Who told you I was back? Meg Stanbridge?'

'Yes, I believe it was.'

'Remind me to strangle her next time I see her.'

'Oh I don't think that's very Christian of you, Ivy. Although I must confess to having felt the same inclination once or twice. But please don't tell anyone.' He winked and smiled.

'Your secret's safe with me. Are you off to watch The Hideaway Hoppers? I saw Bartram and the rest of them earlier. I hear the May Queen has a ring through her nose.'

'I see you're catching up on village gossip, Ivy. Anything I've missed?'

Ivy grinned. Kevin Longbourne was without doubt the nicest vicar Hideaway Down had ever had.

'Did you know we've got a real-life Hollywood actor in town? His name's Jamie McDay. He plays a vampire called Adam in a movie blockbuster series amusingly entitled *Keep a Lid on It* – the 'It' being Adam. At least he did. Rumour has it that he punched some big Hollywood honcho and the paparazzi are posting all sorts of pictures of him. They're saying he may be dropped from the fourth film.'

'Good heavens. No, I didn't. That will no doubt cause some excitement in the village, and there's quite a lot of that already with all the May Day celebrations and whatnot. I'll have to keep my eye on him.'

'Er… you're not going to try and run him out of the village with a crucifix and holy water, are you?'

The Reverend laughed. 'Only if he starts biting my flock.'

'Well, he can bite me any time.'

'Hmm. I'm not sure you should let Ned hear you say that.'

'Oh God! Don't you start. Oops. Sorry, vicar.'

He touched her shoulder with one hand and gave her a friendly smile. 'Some things will probably never change in Hideaway Down. Well, I had better be off. You take care, Ivy. No doubt I'll see you this afternoon for the May Queen crowning, or perhaps I'll see you in church on

Sunday?'

'Yeah right. As you said, vicar, "Some things will probably never change," and me not going to church on Sunday is one of them. See ya.'

She wasn't sure whether she should laugh or cry as she walked towards the footpath and the stile leading up towards Hideaway Cliff and Holly's cottage. She had left her car in the car park behind the shops on Market Street, having decided that a walk in the fresh air would do her good, especially on such a lovely day. Now she wasn't so sure. Why did everyone keep telling her that she mustn't let Ned hear her say she fancied Jamie? Surely they knew she wasn't serious? And even if she was, Ned didn't own her. They'd only been dating since Christmas. What was wrong with people? And wasn't it better to be honest in any case?

Besides, it wasn't as if anything was going to happen between her and Jamie. He was a Hollywood superstar; she was an executive assistant in London. The only thing they had in common was the fact that they both knew famous people... and Gabriel. And she loved Ned, so even if some fairy godmother, or, as it was May Day weekend, some pagan white witch, cast a spell on Jamie and made him fall madly in love with her, she would have to say: 'Thanks, but I have a boyfriend.'

Wouldn't she? Of course she would. She loved Ned. She *really* loved Ned. What she didn't love was being lectured. Another thing she didn't love – and perhaps she should give this one some serious thought – was the prospect of spending the rest of her life living in Hideaway Down, married to the local blacksmith. No matter how kind or thoughtful, gorgeous or sexy, or how sensational in bed, he was. Because one of the things she knew for certain was that Ned Stelling, much like her sister, Holly, would never leave this village, no matter what.

Chapter Eight

Jamie yawned and stretched his arms above his head as he ambled into the kitchen of Holly Cottage, wearing only his boxer shorts and the T-shirt he had worn since leaving L.A. yesterday. He had slept a little on the overnight flight but he was exhausted and had been hoping to sleep for more than just a couple of hours when Gabriel had brought him back here earlier. The thing was, he was used to the total darkness provided by his blackout shutters in his own home in Hollywood, and the minute he saw the sunlight bouncing off the pink and white rosebud walls, curtains and bedding, he knew there would be a problem. Even with the curtains tightly closed, yellow-gold light filled the twee bedroom and no matter how he positioned himself in the otherwise comfy bed, or placed a pillow over his head, he could not hide from the brightness.

'If that's coffee I can smell, Holly, I could murder a cup. Strong and black. Where's Gabriel? I didn't hear you arrive.'

The stunning girl who turned to face him wasn't Holly… was she? Apart from the photos Gabriel had emailed him, he had only seen Holly in the flesh this morning but he was sure this wasn't her. She looked similar but there was something about this girl that made him do a double take. And that hadn't happened when he had met Holly in the café. Holly was pretty, definitely, but this girl… Wow! And that smile. Je-sus. Men would fight vampires to see a smile like that. Then there were her eyes. Had he ever seen eyes that green? Or that gorgeous?

He couldn't look away.

What was happening to him? Beautiful women were everywhere back in L.A. but none of them made him feel like this. Not even Perdita – and she was the hottest thing he'd seen in years. He couldn't move. He couldn't speak. But neither could she, it seemed. He didn't care. He would happily spend the rest of the day just standing here, staring at her.

That thought made him smile. That was dramatic, even for him.

He coughed, attempted to speak and coughed again. The stunner beat him to it.

'I... I'm not Holly. I'm her twin sister, Ivy. We're not identical twins but we do look very alike – especially from the back.' She smiled again. 'You must think I'm an idiot for staring at you like this, but the truth is, I'm a huge fan. This is such a thrill for me. I'm not normally lost for words. Ask anyone. They usually want me to shut up. I... I don't suppose there's any chance that I could take a picture of us together, is there?' She rummaged in her handbag and pulled out her phone.

Did she just say that he must think *she's* an idiot? He was the only idiot around here.

'Sure. No problem... Ivy' Even her name sounded good on his tongue. 'Shall I come over there?' Could he walk? He stepped forward. Thank God for that.

'I... I can't believe you're a friend of Gabriel's. Or that he didn't tell us. Are you staying long?'

'That depends.'

'Oh! On what?'

'Well, for one thing, whether I have a job to go back to.'

He stood next to her and placed an arm around her waist, pulling her close to his side.

'Don't you think you will?' Ivy took the photo just as he looked at her profile. 'Oh, you looked away. May I take another?'

'You can take as many as you want.' He pulled her closer and leant his cheek against hers. 'Is this better?' It definitely was for him.

'Th... that's great. Thanks so much. You must get sick of people asking you to do this.'

'Take another. Just in case. And you can ask me as often as you like.'

She took three more and finally eased away from him. He tried to think of a reason not to let her go but he couldn't. Well, not one that wouldn't make her want to run for the hills, thinking he was five different types of lunatic. He was beginning to think that himself.

Ivy gave him an odd look. 'You were saying... about your job.'

'Oh right. Yeah. There's a very strong possibility that I've been canned. I mean I think I may have been dropped from the next film.'

She suddenly smiled. 'Don't you mean coffined? After all, you do play the role of a vampire. Sorry. That wasn't funny.'

Jamie laughed. 'Actually it was. Yeah, I've been coffined. They've finally put a lid on *It*. And the chances are, they plan to keep it tightly closed.'

'But how can they? You're the star. You're *It*. You're Adam. Without you there is no *It*.'

'In Hollywood, there's always a way. They'll either find a lookalike and kill me off in the first five seconds of the next film, or they'll keep their – and my – options open and make up some storyline where I've gone off to contemplate the real meaning of my life... or death, as I'm technically dead.'

'Well, I think they'd be crazy to write you out. And your fans will be up in arms. I know I would be.'

'Would you be…?' He managed to stop himself in time. He had almost asked if she would be up in *his* arms. Right now. Right this second.

He must be seriously jetlagged. There was no other explanation for it. Yes, she was beautiful. But he'd seen 'beautiful' thousands of times and none of them had made him feel this way as far as he could remember.

'Would I be…?' she coaxed.

His mind raced. 'Er… Would you be making a cup of coffee, by any chance? I think I'm suffering from jetlag and I could really use the caffeine.'

'Yes, of course. Sorry. Sit down and I'll make you one. Strong and black I think you said, but I was so busy staring at you when you came in just now, I'm not really sure I heard you correctly. Oh. I think that's Holly and Gabriel arriving. I'd assumed they were already here but they must have gone somewhere else in the village when they left the shop. Sorry, I'm rambling. I still can't believe I'm in my sister's kitchen with Jamie McDay.'

'Neither can I.'

She giggled; nervously it seemed to him.

'No. This must seem very strange after what you've been used to in Hollywood. I expect your kitchen is bigger than these four cottages put together.'

'You're right. My kitchen's huge. But as I don't cook, I'm hardly ever in there. And right now, I'd rather be in this kitchen any day.'

'Oh!' Holly walked in, took one look at him, looked over at her sister and then glared at Jamie.

What had he done to upset her because she was clearly upset? He was about to ask when Gabriel came in and stopped in his tracks.

'Jesus, Jamie! Put some clothes on, will you? This isn't... Ivy? What're you doing here? What's going on?'

Jamie had forgotten he was only wearing boxers and a T-shirt. And Gabriel knew what he was like with women. His friend was obviously putting two and two together and getting several shades of sex.

'Nothing's going on,' Ivy said. 'I thought you were here because you weren't at the shop. Jamie came down from upstairs and thought I was Holly. I mean, he thought I was making coffee. Which I am. Making coffee. D'you want some?'

'Really?' Gabriel looked at Ivy, then at Jamie and back at Ivy. 'And neither of you thought it might be a good idea for Jamie to put some clothes on?'

'Why?' Ivy sounded indignant. 'I've seen men in boxer shorts before, Gabriel. I mean, he's hardly naked, is he?'

Holly frowned. 'I'm not sure Ned would see it like that.'

'Oh, for heaven's sake! Will you all stop telling me what Ned will and won't see, or like, or feel, or say? I'm getting really sick of it. I think I'll go to Laurel's for coffee. Jamie – would you like to come with me?'

'I'd love to. But I'd better get some clothes on first. Give me two minutes and I'm all yours.'

'Don't let Ned hear you say that,' Gabriel said, as Jamie turned to go upstairs. 'Sorry, Ivy, but Jamie might be the one being punched if he does. Instead of being the one doing the punching.'

Ivy tutted. 'Don't be so ridiculous. Ned wouldn't hit anyone. Oh! I didn't mean... Jamie, that wasn't a reflection on you hitting... I mean... I think I'll stop talking.'

Jamie smiled. 'That's okay, Ivy. It was a spectacularly dumb thing to do, even for me, and I've done some pretty dumb things in my time. But… who's Ned? I'm sure I heard that name in the coffee shop this morning.'

Holly glowered at him. 'Ned is Ivy's boyfriend. And the local blacksmith.'

Jamie felt as if he *had* been punched. 'Your boyfriend? You've got a boyfriend? Of course you've got a boyfriend. Why am I so surprised by that? Is it serious? Have you been together long?'

Ivy met his look. 'I… I suppose it is. I mean… I do love him. But no, we've only been together since Christmas.'

'But you've known him all your life!' Holly was obviously annoyed. She threw Jamie a look to kill. 'Ivy and Ned were made for each other.'

Jamie pulled himself together. This was a blow. But not one he couldn't recover from. So Ivy had a boyfriend. So what? That meant nothing. Boyfriends – and girlfriends for that matter – came and went. Holly was being an idiot. No one was *made* for someone else.

'Well, if they were made for one another,' he said, smiling at Holly and Gabriel, 'having coffee with me isn't going to change that, is it?' He raced upstairs to get dressed. And to think of a way to get Ivy away from Ned without annoying Gabriel and Holly. After all, Ivy clearly wasn't head over heels in love with this Ned guy. If she was, she wouldn't have hesitated when she'd said it.

Coming to Hideaway Down might turn out to be one of his better decisions, and he hadn't made a lot of good decisions lately. Punching Rod Finer definitely hadn't been a good idea, even if it had given him a great deal of satisfaction at the time. He hadn't thought it through and as usual he'd acted on the spur of the moment – something Gabriel and Gabriel's gran, Gabriella often warned him about in his early days as a struggling actor. Too late to worry about that now. "What's done is done," as Gabriella would have said if she were here today. "There's no point in crying over spilt milk."

She was right, and she used to say something else, too: "Life is short. Make hay whilst the sun shines."

Well, the sun was certainly shining and he would make as much hay as he could. Yes, coming to Hideaway Down was definitely a good decision. And it looked as though it might be a whole lot more fun than he had ever imagined.

Now what was he going to do about Ned?

Chapter Nine

Ned was *not* in a good mood. He generally considered himself to be a fairly happy-go-lucky, easy going sort of guy but since Christmas, it wasn't just his mother, Audrey, who had noticed a change in him. Now he seemed to swing from one strange mood to another, often in a matter of minutes. Was it something to do with him dating Ivy? He would be the first to admit that he spent an inordinate amount of time either thinking about her, worrying about her, missing her or, as on days like this, being downright annoyed with her.

Take this morning for example. When he'd gone to get his coffee at Laurel's he'd been feeling like a kid at Christmas. Ivy was coming home for a long weekend and he'd arranged a special picnic lunch, hoping to spend some quality, romantic time with her. He was counting the minutes until she arrived, especially after she phoned him from the motorway to say that she would be arriving early. After telling her to drive safely, he'd found it difficult to concentrate on his work and he assumed she would be as eager to see him as he was to see her. But apparently, he was wrong. She went to see half the village before she turned up at his door.

Okay, perhaps that was a slight exaggeration, and he shouldn't really moan simply because his girlfriend wanted to go and say a quick hello to her sister, and then grab a cup of coffee before coming to see him. But even so, when Meg Stanbridge gave him the news of Ivy's whereabouts, his heart deflated like a three-day-old party balloon.

And things then went from bad to worse. No romantic, picnic lunch for them, oh no. Ivy wanted to go to the pub to see some actor-guy instead. And what Ivy wanted, Ivy invariably got. There was no point in telling her what he'd planned, although he did try. But he realised that would only make her feel guilty and then she'd have to choose. He didn't want that. He wanted her to be happy. He would do anything he could to see that gorgeous smile of hers. Anything to witness the twinkle in her emerald green eyes.

So instead of telling her about the picnic and his plans, he'd agreed to meet her in the pub. What he really should have done, was shut up shop for fifteen minutes as she'd suggested. He wanted to. He wanted to so badly. Would it have been such a crime?

But no, he'd stupidly put his customers first and irrationally decided it was okay to close for an hour for lunch but not for a fifteen-minute coffee break to show his gorgeous girlfriend just how much he'd missed her. Oh no. Not him. He was a total idiot at times. He seemed to spend half his life these days trying to think of ways to make Ivy happy and when he gets the chance, like today, he fails completely.

It was his own fault; he had no one else to blame. Not even Ivy. He'd known what she was like long before they got together romantically. They'd been friends for most of their lives; good friends and he probably knew her almost as well as anyone did. And everyone knew one thing for certain about Ivy: you could never be sure what she was going to do next. If he were honest, that was one of the things he loved about her. She was unpredictable; she was spontaneous; she was carefree; she was fun and sometimes, like today, she was bloody annoying.

But in truth, was he annoyed with her, or with himself?

He and Ivy were like chalk and cheese in many ways. She loved the bright lights of London; he loved the dark nights and the starlit skies of Hideaway Down. She got a thrill out of meeting famous people and drinking vintage champagne at some big celebrity bash; he got pleasure in going to The Snowdrop Inn and chatting with the regulars over a pint from the local brewery.

When they'd got together at Christmas, he'd been as surprised by it as she was, although he'd been secretly in love with her for almost his entire life. If anyone else in the village was surprised, they didn't say much about it. "Always knew you two would get together," was the general consensus – even from his mum. Although Audrey had added a caveat:

'Well, it was a toss-up between Ivy and Laurel, as far as I was concerned,' Audrey had said. 'I suppose I'm not surprised that it's Ivy who's won your heart. But she's a real live-wire, that one. You just make sure you don't get burnt.'

Ned frowned at the memory; just as he'd frowned when his mum had spoken those words. For one thing, he knew there was a very good chance that he might get his heart broken by Ivy Gilroy; he didn't need his mother to point that out. For another… Laurel? Why on earth would his mum think there was a chance he might end up with Laurel? All Audrey would say at the time was that "it didn't matter. You've chosen Ivy and that's that". She hadn't elaborated and he hadn't questioned her further. It didn't matter she was right. He *had* chosen Ivy and he was over the moon about it.

But thinking of getting burnt, he wondered if Laurel's fingers were still hurting. Scalds could be very painful things.

'Hello handsome. I see you've got something hard and

hot in your hands. Are you pleased to see me?'

Ned recognised the voice and grinned. 'Hello Shauna.' He placed the workpiece in the water, tossed the tongs and hammer on the bench and wiped his hands before turning to face her and her three friends. 'You're looking well as always. What can I interest you in today?'

She tottered towards him wearing ridiculously high heels as usual. She was a frequent customer and several times in the past she'd stumbled on the uneven floor. If he hadn't managed to catch her in his arms in time, she would have landed flat on her face on concrete instead of face first against his chest.

'Oh Ned. You know the only thing I'm truly interested in is you, you sexy hunk.'

He coughed and dragged a hand through his hair. She was teasing, he knew that, but even so her flirtatious behaviour, risqué comments and double entendres, made him a little uncomfortable sometimes. He wasn't altogether certain how to respond. She was a good-looking woman but she was probably the same age as his mother and that was... well... he wasn't really into the whole 'cougar' thing.

'I wish my girlfriend felt the same way.'

'Your girlfriend? Having relationship problems, are we? I'm a very good listener, you know and what I haven't done isn't worth doing. I can give you some tips to put the sizzle back if that's the problem. Although just looking at you makes *me* sizzle, so I can't believe sex is the issue. Unless you're not getting enough of it for your liking. I can help you with that too. Come to Shauna!'

She stretched out her arms and beckoned him to her with her index finger. The sight of the long red-painted nail sent a strange sensation down his spine and for one brief second, he wasn't sure whether it was a shiver of dread or a quiver of delight. Good God! What was wrong with him? He definitely should have shut up shop and had that fifteen-minute romp with Ivy.

'Thanks for the offer, but I don't think I could handle you.' He smiled and forced a wink. Keep it light-hearted, he told himself.

'Oh honey, you can handle me anytime. And I promise you, you won't regret it.'

'Shauna! Leave the poor man alone.'

One of the friends whose name Ned couldn't recall for the life of him, stepped in to his rescue. Shauna pouted and used that same red nail to trace a circle around the excessively low neckline of her top.

'I haven't touched him... yet.'

'Are you going to the May Day Market?' Ned attempted to change the subject.

'Yes,' the friend said. 'And to watch the crowning of the May Queen.'

'I was a Beauty Queen, you know,' Shauna said. 'It was a few years ago now but I was a real stunner. I think I still look pretty good, even if I say so myself. Do you think I look good, handsome?'

'I think... I think you all look great. My girlfriend was the May Queen once and everyone in the village still says she was the prettiest Queen we've ever had. She's absolutely gorgeous. She's home this weekend and I can't wait to spend some time with her. So much so that I'm closing for lunch at twelve. So, ladies. Is there anything that takes your fancy?' He threw Shauna a look. 'Apart from me that is, Shauna. Because, sadly, I'm already well and truly taken. And I would never, ever, cheat on the woman I love.'

Chapter Ten

Laurel was surprised to see Ivy walk into The Coffee Hideaway for a second time this morning, especially as it was only a little over an hour since she had left the first time. Laurel was even more surprised to see that Ivy was accompanied by none other than Jamie McDay. But what surprised her the most was the large, decidedly purple bruise on Jamie's jaw.

Laurel stifled a laugh as he edged his way towards the counter. The café was packed and his progress was slow, allowing her ample time to study his face once Ivy had taken a seat at a table a young couple had that minute, vacated. Laurel returned Ivy's wave and resumed her scrutiny of Jamie. Not only was his face bruised but his dark hair, so black and shiny earlier, was somewhat dishevelled, with traces of what looked like mud in it. His black leather jacket also bore brown patches as did his jeans. Was he limping? He definitely looked grumpier than he had first thing this morning.

'What happened to you?' Laurel shot a look past him towards Ivy but she was now staring out into the crowds on Market Street.

'No one punched me, if that's what you're thinking, but there's a damn good chance I've got a broken jaw, so that must make you smile.'

'It doesn't. Soooo… are you going to tell me or do I have to guess?'

He frowned, reached up to touch his jaw, then rubbed his hand over his hair and glanced at his palm. It was smeared with mud.

'Let's just say, I had an altercation with a stile. Ivy said you might be good enough to let me wash up in your bathroom. It's only mud. Nothing more disgusting. At least I hope not.'

'Wash up? Oh, you mean clean yourself up. For a moment I thought you were offering to do the dishes. Sorry. I shouldn't make fun of you. Are you hurt?'

'Only my pride.' He glanced down at his feet. 'Wrong shoes for country rambles. I'd better get myself a pair of hiking boots if I'm going to stay around here. Although why everyone wants to walk rather than use a car, is beyond my comprehension.'

'You're not in Hollywood now. People walk in Hideaway Down. It might do you good to do some walking. It'll put some colour in your cheeks.'

He blinked several times. 'Seriously? Put some colour in my cheeks? You sound like Gabriel's gran used to. The only thing it's put colour in so far is my hair and my clothes. So... bathroom?'

Laurel grinned. 'Through that door on the right, up the stairs and it's the second door to your right at the top. You'll find clean towels in the tall cupboard near the bath. Throw the ones you use in the empty bath when you've finished. I'll put them in the washing machine later.'

'Thanks. You're a lifesaver. I owe you one.' He moved towards the door Laurel had indicated but stopped, his fingers holding it open. 'Oh. Ivy would like her usual, whatever that is and I'd like...' A hint of a smile curved his lips. 'I'd like a *Laurel's*, please. I still want to know what *that* tastes like.' He winked and disappeared up the stairs.

Laurel stared at the door as it slowly closed behind him on its automatic hinge. Still flirting then. Perhaps it came with the territory. Everyone in Hollywood probably did it, or some form of it, but they no doubt called it networking in LA-LA-land.

She turned away and made Ivy's cappuccino. She then poured freshly brewed coffee into a large cup for Jamie, placing them on a tray together with petite jugs of milk and cream, and a bowl of sugar. She carried the tray to Ivy's table and perched on the seat opposite her, leaning her elbows on the table and grinning.

'I'm surprised to see you back here. Especially with him. Did he fall or did you push him?'

Ivy gave her a startled look, as if she were miles away and hadn't noticed Laurel's approach.

'What? Oh, he fell. I warned him that the stile might be slippery. He helped me over and he seemed fine but when I looked back, he was flying backwards through the air. I couldn't reach him in time and he landed in the mud. He said he'd caught his foot on the top bar or something.' Ivy giggled. 'It wasn't really funny. He could've hurt himself, but I couldn't resist making some comment about him not being very bat-like, for a vampire. And then I started singing *Catch A Falling Star*, and I think it annoyed him.'

Laurel laughed. 'So naturally you sang it all the more.'

Ivy shrugged. 'I couldn't help it. Even superstars come down to earth with a bump, it seems. You don't mind me offering him your bathroom, do you? You were the nearest.'

'No, I don't mind. He wasn't terribly amused when he asked to "wash up" and I told him I thought he was offering to do the dishes, either. I don't think he's got a very good sense of humour.'

'Americans don't understand British sarcasm. But then again, he's not American. He's English. Oh well. He'll soon get used to it if he stays any length of time in

Hideaway Down.'

'You don't seem quite as in awe of him as you sounded earlier. Has the star fallen in more ways than one?'

'No way! He's still gorgeous and I'm still his biggest fan. I'm just not in a very good mood, that's all. It's not because of him though. Well, perhaps in a way it is.'

'I don't follow you.'

Ivy looked Laurel straight in the eye. 'It's Ned.'

'Ned?' Laurel swallowed the lump in her throat.

Ivy nodded. 'Everyone keeps telling me what Ned would and wouldn't like, or what I should and shouldn't do. I've only been home for a couple of hours and I feel as if I've stepped into some version of *The Stepford Wives*. I'm sick of it already. Ned doesn't own me and I don't own him. Sorry. I shouldn't be dumping this on you.' She sighed deeply and took a large gulp of her coffee, staring out into Market Street again.

'There's no need to be sorry, Ivy. We may not see each other very often but you can tell me anything. You know that. Are you… are you saying that you're having doubts about you and Ned?'

Ivy shot her a look. 'No! I'm… I'm not really sure what I *am* saying. Just ignore me. I'm tired. I didn't get to bed until gone three this morning and then Mum woke me at what felt like the crack of dawn to tell me about Jamie. I got in the car and drove straight here. What I really need is some sleep.'

'You and me both,' Jamie said. 'Thanks for letting me use your bathroom. I've left the towel in the bath as you said, but I did rinse it out because it was pretty muddy.'

Laurel was surprised. Firstly, because she hadn't noticed his return and secondly, because he had bothered to rinse out the towel he'd used. Perhaps he wasn't quite as bad as she had first thought. Perhaps he had some manners, after all.

The bruise appeared to have increased in proportion but all other traces of his mishap had been removed. His black hair glinted under the glow from the ceiling lights and the leather jacket was spotless once again, although there were a couple of damp patches on his jeans where he had washed off the mud.

Laurel stood up and smiled down at Ivy. 'Well, there's not going to be much chance of that today what with everything going on. And I see I'm wanted by some customers. Catch you later.'

So it wasn't all rosy in Ivy and Ned's garden. Laurel should be pleased but she wasn't. Ivy meant so much to Ned. He would be heartbroken if they split up. And as much as she wanted Ned, she didn't want to see him hurt.

How would he feel when he heard that Ivy and Jamie were having coffee together? And *he* would hear. Someone in the village would tell him. Would he mind? Would he be jealous? Was there reason for him to be? It was just coffee, after all. There was nothing wrong with two people having coffee together. Even if one of them was a handsome Hollywood superstar and the other, his biggest fan.

Or should that be: fallen Hollywood superstar? Because he wasn't really handsome… was he? Appealing, yes, but handsome…? Hmm. She hadn't thought so this morning but now there was definitely something about him. She merely couldn't decide what. And now she would be humming *Catch A Falling Star* all day. Well, thank you very much, Ivy Gilroy.

Chapter Eleven

'So this is The Snowdrop Inn?'

Jamie surveyed the late fifteenth-, early sixteenth-century, slightly askew façade, and smiled. It was the perfect, picture-postcard pub. The long, two-storey building stood back from Market Street on a raised bank of grass which sloped down to a pond on one side; not large but big enough for several families of ducks to paddle happily about. Beyond the pond lay a huge field, fenced off from a narrow pavement. There was a sign saying: 'Market Field' in large iron letters on an intricately designed iron gate – clearly the work of a very talented blacksmith. Hadn't Holly told him that Ivy's boyfriend was a blacksmith? The gate faced the pond but it needed no sign to indicate its use; the field was packed with market stalls and noisy, happy shoppers. This must be the May Day Market he had heard so much about, not that he was interested in markets.

'I'm dying for a pint of good old English beer. You can't get one in L.A. no matter what some publicans try to tell you.'

Ivy smiled. 'You're in luck. This place serves the best local ales and the biggest selection in the county. My mum owns it, so make sure you're on your best behaviour.'

'Your mum owns a pub and you're the most beautiful woman I've ever seen!' Jamie winked and smiled. 'I think I'm in love.'

Ivy flushed scarlet. 'Say that inside and you're likely to find yourself in the pond. Mum is a big fan of my boyfriend. Come on. Let's get you that pint.'

Jamie followed Ivy towards the black plank door, past wooden tables and chairs dotted higgledy-piggledy around the frontage, some of which were already occupied by smiling customers. One young couple sat arm in arm leaning against an ancient chestnut tree, easily recognisable by its pointed palmate leaves and the shiny oval, dark red buds, sticky to the touch. A few blossoms were beginning to open, the white fringed petals and the pink blush at the base, clearly visible. It was one of Jamie's favourite trees and his smile widened as a hundred childhood memories flooded his brain and the scent of someone, somewhere, cutting grass, filled his nostrils.

'The Hollywood bods would love this. It's the perfect setting for a film. Mind you, they'd probably want to set it on fire or blow it up. Well, at least a replica of it.'

'Mum would love that! She adores this place and if someone so much as scratches their initials in that tree they would soon find themselves hanging from its branches by a rope.'

Ivy pushed open the door to the sound of tinkling bells on the overhead beam.

'It just gets better and better.'

'Are you being sarcastic?' Ivy gave him a stern look.

'No. Honestly I'm not. I love it. It's been a long time since I've enjoyed a pint in a place like this. And I mean that in a good way.'

Two large, log fires burned brightly at either end of the pub, in spite of the fact that it was a warm and sunny day, and mouth-watering smells wafted in from somewhere behind the bar, at which a row of people perched on high, wooden stools, chatted happily.

Jamie slipped off his jacket. 'It's warm in here.'

Ivy did the same. 'Yeah. Gramps – that's my

grandfather – says there should be a fire in the hearth until at least the first of June. Mind you, if last summer was anything to go by, there'll be a fire virtually every day of the year. It did almost nothing but rain last year, especially in the autumn. But it was fabulous at Christmas. Market Field was flooded and the water froze. We had a frost fair on the ice. It was spectacular and I think I'll remember it for the rest of my life. Bloody cold though.'

'I would like to have seen that. I remember Gabriel telling me about it.'

'Oh? What else did Gabriel tell you?'

'What he *didn't* tell me was that someone as beautiful as you lived here. If he had, I would have been on the first plane over.'

Ivy blushed again. 'I don't live here. I live in London.'

'Seriously? And yet… doesn't your boyfriend live in the village? I know London's not that far away but it must be difficult to maintain a good relationship. Or am I completely wrong?'

Ivy looked at him from beneath her lashes. 'It's not… easy. But I love Ned and he loves me.'

'I don't doubt for a minute that he loves you. He'd be a fool not to. One look at you and I was completely lost.'

'Stop flirting with me. I know you're only teasing but this village is full of gossips. If someone hears you say stuff like that, the next thing you'll hear is that we're running off together.'

'That sounds good to me.'

Ivy tutted. 'Stop it!'

'Seriously, Ivy. Would that be so bad? And for your information, I'm not teasing.'

He held her gaze for what seemed to him like several minutes but in reality was probably only a matter of seconds before someone called her name and she turned away.

'Ivy! Coo-ey.'

'Hi, Mum.' Ivy dashed forward and threw herself into her mother's arms.

'Don't tell me you've only just arrived, darling?'

Ivy shook her head as she eased herself away. 'No. I got here a couple of hours ago. I popped in to see Holly, grabbed a coffee, went to see Ned, and then... in a roundabout way, came here.'

'Oh so your mum's last on your list, eh? That's lovely, isn't it?' Despite her words, she smiled.

'You're last because you're the most important. Well, you and Gramps. And Merlot and Mistletoe, of course.'

'Of course. It's nice to know your grandfather and I rank equally with the dog and cat. And who's this handsome but I have to say, rather pale-looking young man? Are you the Hollywood star we've all been hearing about? You need to get some sun on your face, if you don't mind me saying. I'm Janet. Janet Gilroy, Ivy's mum but you've probably already guessed that. You can call me Janet.'

Jamie grinned and held out his hand. 'I'm very pleased to meet you, Janet. And you can say anything you like. I can see where Ivy gets her looks from.'

Janet pulled an amused face. 'Compliments, eh? That's a good start, I suppose. Can I get you a pint of beer? And possibly... some fake tan? I'm sure I've got some somewhere.'

Ivy laughed. 'She's joking. But you'd better get used to it. You'll probably get a lot of that in Hideaway Down.'

'That's fine with me. And yes, please... to both the pint and the fake tan. It might help me blend in with the locals.'

Janet grinned and slapped him on the arm. 'I like you,

Jamie McDay. You're my kind of man. Not into older women by any chance? I could do with a toy boy right now. Especially a famous one. Oh, would it get me on the cover of one of those celebrity-gossip magazines?'

Jamie nodded. 'Very likely. But I've fallen from favour at the moment so you might not want to have your photo linked with mine.'

'A bad boy, eh? Ooh. I like you more and more by the minute.'

'Mum! Will you behave? He might think you're serious.'

Janet laughed. 'He's knows I'm not. What is wrong with you today, darling? You don't seem quite your usual, cheerful self. You haven't had a row with Ned, have you? Where he is by the way? I heard he was taking you on a romantic picnic lunch. He's even bought your favourite stinky cheese. That must be love.'

'He's what?' Ivy looked mortified. 'A picnic? He was planning to take me on a picnic?'

Janet shook her head. 'I know. Daft thing to do on the last day of April. Picnics are summer things. But I suppose he thought that with all the nice weather we've been having recently, it was a good idea. And Hideaway Hole will be quiet today. Everyone'll be in the village. So it would be rather romantic. Apart from the stinking cheese, in my opinion. Hold on. What do you mean by "was"? You are still going, aren't you? Didn't he tell you? Maisy told me he's ordered bread and cakes and everything.'

Jamie didn't like the expression on Ivy's face. He didn't like it one bit. She looked as if she might burst into tears.

He tipped his head to one side to get a better look. 'Are you okay?'

She stared at him. 'No I'm not. I... I had no idea that Ned had planned a picnic. When he said he wanted to do something special for lunch I thought he meant...' She blushed profusely, glancing from him to her mum. 'It doesn't matter what I thought. The point is, I told him I wanted to come here and have lunch with you instead. No wonder he wasn't very happy. Oh God! Sorry, Jamie. Sorry, Mum. I've got to go.'

'Too late for that, darling. Ned's just walked in and he's heading this way.'

Jamie and Ivy both turned to face the door. No way. It was the guy he'd bumped into at The Coffee Hideaway this morning. The one he thought was ogling Laurel. Well, well. This explained a lot. For a moment there he'd thought all hope was lost.

Now, there was a chance. Okay, it was a very small chance but he had seen the way Ned looked at Laurel and the way she looked at Ned. Jamie had acted the part of a star-crossed lover and also the part of a guy in love with someone and not realising it until it was almost too late. He'd also played the part of the male friend slowly falling for the female friend. The Ned slash Laurel scenario was a combination of all of those roles. He was sure of that. Perhaps, if he could somehow bring Ned and Laurel closer, it might work out to everyone's advantage. It would certainly work out to his.

'You came!' Ivy sounded like a mouse.

Ned frowned but when she ran to him and threw her arms around his neck, a huge smile spread across his face.

'Of course I did.' Ned wrapped his arms around her and pulled her close.

Jamie watched them for a moment. He'd have to set to work pretty quickly. He would think of it as a project. Perhaps he should give it a pet name just as the media would; a name like… Naurel. Yes. That amused him. He grinned. Why had he thought that coming to Hideaway Down would be boring? So far it had been anything but. He turned his attention to Janet as she placed a pint of beer on the bar.

She nodded in the direction of Ned and Ivy and smiled. 'They make a lovely couple, don't they?'

Ned took a sip of his drink. 'God, that's good, Janet. Thanks. So that's Ned? It's a funny thing, you know. When I arrived this morning at a little after seven-thirty, he was just leaving The Coffee Hideaway and he and Laurel, that lovely girl who owns—'

'I know who Laurel is. What were you saying about her and Ned?'

'Of course you do. She lives right here in this cosy little village. I was only saying, that I thought they were boyfriend and girlfriend.'

'Ned and Laurel? Why? What on earth would make you think that?'

'Well, partly because it was so early and he was leaving as I arrived, and he was lingering in the doorway, saying a gushing goodbye. And partly because I thought they were looking at one another like love-sick cows, but clearly I was mistaken. Did they once go out together? Is there history between them?'

'Laurel and Ned? No. They've never dated. They've known each other all their lives though. Just like they've known Ivy and Holly. They all grew up together. Played together. Went to school together. They're all friends because they're all around the same age. They're very close.'

'Ah. That must be it then. They certainly looked close.' He took another quick sip. 'Only I could have sworn…' He shrugged, symbolically he hoped.

Janet stiffened. 'Could have sworn what?'

'Oh... nothing. Ignore me. What do I know? I'm a stranger here and know nothing of the intricacies of village relationships. And he and Laurel must see a lot of each other. I expect he's always popping in and out for coffee, and what with Ivy living in London, well, it's probably good to have such a friendly face nearby, especially someone you've been very close to all your life.'

Janet leant her elbows on the bar, crossed her arms and looked him in the eye. 'I like you, Jamie. Don't make me think I've made a mistake to do so.'

'I like you, too, Janet. And perhaps I'm being thick, or perhaps it's the jetlag but I don't know what you mean.'

'Hmm. You may be jetlagged but you're not thick. You know it as well as I do. And I saw the way you looked at Ivy earlier, so let me be clear. I love my daughter very much and no one, no one at all is going to break my daughter's heart without expecting me to do something about it.'

'I understand perfectly, Janet. But I'm not sure what you think I could do to break your daughter's heart. I wasn't the one staring all doe-eyed at Laurel this morning. I think you may be having this conversation with the wrong man. But I'll tell you what. I'm happy to ask Laurel out if you think that might help. Would it? Unless she already has a boyfriend. Does she?'

'No. She doesn't as it happens.'

'Awesome. She's not into celebrities. She's already made that perfectly clear and I'm sure I'm not the first red-blooded male to notice that she's pretty damned hot but I'm willing to make a fool of myself and risk rejection. There's nothing quite as attractive as a beautiful girl who's happy in her own space and isn't in the least bit star-struck. Plus, I'm partial to women on the 'cuddly' side. In fact, the more I think about Laurel, the more I can't believe that some local guy, like Ned for example, hasn't snapped her up.'

'Ned loves Ivy. He's always loved Ivy. It just took him a while to see it.'

'Great. Then I won't have any competition for Laurel, will I? Because Ivy was telling me that there're hardly any people in our age group living here, which is one of the reasons she finds the village rather boring compared to London. Well, that and the lack of nightlife. Ivy said she likes to party. Is Ned a party animal? I don't think Laurel is. I'll have to ask her. Perhaps the four of us can go to a nightclub in Eastbourne if they are. Ivy says that's the nearest one.'

Janet narrowed her eyes. 'You're a smart one, aren't you? It makes me wonder why you did something so stupid as to punch the studio boss and get yourself arrested if you know how to 'play' people so well.'

Jamie grinned. She'd understood exactly what he was saying but he wasn't sure she liked it.

'Ah that. We're all idiots sometimes, Janet. It turned out that Perdita, my co-star and girlfriend had, shall we say, reached an understanding with Rod Finer, the head of the studio. It was an understanding that I didn't... understand. Or like. The casting couch is alive and kicking, it seems. It's just taken on a new form. She saw him every Tuesday and Thursday and he gave her, amongst other things, a massive, movie deal. So, as the level-headed guy I am, I got drunk, turned up at a party and dumped her in a loud and public display. Then I punched Finer in the face. Not one of my best performances, I admit, but it felt good at the time. It was hushed up, although not completely, and all charges were dropped. My agent thought it was the perfect time for me to visit my friends in the UK. So here I am.'

Janet stood upright. 'Yes. Here you are. And let me give you some free advice. I suggest you learn from that experience. There are no casting couches in Hideaway Down, in any way, shape or form. You're not in Hollywood now, remember. Ask Laurel out if you like her, but mess with her heart, or anyone else's and you'll discover how Rod Finer felt. Mess with my daughter's heart and they'll never find your body. Now drink up and let me get you another. It's not often we get a Hollywood star in our village pub. Especially one who I'm pretty certain, is going to cause a whole heap of trouble and I may end up having to bar from the premises.'

Chapter Twelve

Ivy eased herself away from Ned. 'Mum says you were planning to take me on a picnic. Why didn't you tell me?'

'Because you wanted to come here to meet this Jamie McDay guy and I didn't want to make you have to choose. Is that him talking to Janet? I saw him in Laurel's this morning.'

Ivy glanced over her shoulder. 'Yes, that's him. I've already met him.' She looked up into Ned's eyes and, with one fingernail, traced a line from his Adam's Apple down to the V of his T-shirt. 'N-e-d, as you're not in the least bit interested in celebrities and you've closed the smithy for lunch anyway, why don't we go and have this picnic you've planned? Only… it's a bit muddy still in places over the fields, so perhaps we could picnic inside instead.'

'Are you sure? I honestly don't mind if you'd rather we stay here.'

'No Ned. I'd rather have a picnic with you.'

Ned beamed at her. 'Well, there's no need to worry about mud. I've got one of those plastic coated blankets. It's Mum's actually but it's specifically made for occasions like this.'

Ivy drew in a breath. 'Okay. Let me rephrase that. Instead of spending valuable time trudging across potentially muddy fields, why don't we go back to your place, spread this blanket-thing on your bedroom floor and use that time for a much better purpose?'

'Ah. I think I see what you mean. I just thought you might want to be out in the fresh air after being cooped up in an office all week, and then stuck in a car for over an hour to get here. But I'm more than happy to picnic indoors, if you are.'

'I am Ned. Very happy. Besides, fresh air is highly overrated. Give me a sun-filled bedroom over a smithy, followed by a hot shower with a sexy hunk any time.'

'Let's go then. Oh, but shouldn't I just say hi to this Jamie guy? And Janet. They're both giving us really strange looks. It would be rude to just walk out.'

'Only you would think of good manners at a time like this.'

Ned took her hand and headed towards the bar.

'Hi Ned. Usual, is it?' Janet asked.

'Hi, Janet. No thanks. We're not stopping. I just wanted to nip over and say hello.'

Janet raised a hand and waved. 'Great. Have fun you two.' She threw an odd look at Jamie and moved away to serve another customer.

Ned smiled and turned to face Jamie. 'I'm Ned. Ivy's boyfriend. I think we met earlier in The Coffee Hideaway. It's a pleasure to meet you.'

'Yeah, we did. I thought you were Laurel's boyfriend at the time. Good to meet you too. I'm Jamie, but you already know that. So where are you two off to? Going on this picnic I've heard so much about?'

Ned looked surprised. 'How come you've heard about it?'

'Everyone's been making Ivy feel guilty. First Holly, when she found me and Ivy together in the kitchen. Then Laurel, when we went for coffee. And Janet mentioned it the moment we arrived.'

'No, they haven't! That wasn't about the picnic. That was… It doesn't matter. What matters is we're going.' Ivy tugged at Ned's hand. 'Right now, Ned.'

'Bye then. Have a great time.' Jamie raised his pint and smiled.

'Ned.' Ivy tugged harder and virtually dragged Ned towards the door. Judging by the look on his face, she would have some explaining to do.

'What did he mean by "found" you in the kitchen together? And when did you have coffee with him? And more importantly, what has everyone been making you feel guilty about? You only arrived a few hours ago.'

'It's nothing, Ned. There's no need to worry.'

Ned stopped just inside the door, the bells on the overhead beam, tinkling as Ivy opened it.

'Why don't you let me be the judge of that?'

Ivy hated it when Ned gave her that look. He reminded her of Jarvis Pope, her ex-headmaster.

'Let's talk about this at your place.'

She stepped through the open doorway but Ned held back, so she let go of his hand and continued walking. A few seconds later, Ned fell into step beside her and they marched down the grassy bank towards Ned's smithy.

The silence was unbearable but Ivy couldn't think of anything to say to ease the tension she was feeling. She assumed Ned felt the same. How could just a few words spoken by a virtual stranger change their happy mood so quickly?

Ned unlocked the heavy stable door and held it open for Ivy. Once inside, she turned to face him.

'It was nothing, Ned. Honestly. When I left you I went to Holly's shop but she wasn't there so I went to the cottage. Jamie came in when I was making coffee and Holly and Gabriel arrived a few minutes later.'

'And?'

'And nothing. Oh... Holly got annoyed because Jamie didn't have any clothes on because—'

'What?'

Ivy jumped at Ned's tone.

'I mean... he *did* have clothes on. He'd been asleep and just got up, so he wasn't fully dressed. He was completely decent though – T-shirt and boxers. There's nothing wrong with that.'

'I'm not sure I'd agree, but go on.'

'That's it. Holly started giving one of her lectures. I got annoyed. So Jamie and I went to Laurel's for coffee. That's it. Honestly. I told you there was nothing to worry about.'

'Then why did he say that everyone was making you feel guilty?'

Ivy sighed. 'It's silly. People just... well... people have a tendency to tell me that you may or may not like something I've done. Like the way I drive. Or the way I dress. Or the things I say and it annoys me sometimes. And sometimes it makes me feel like I'm a bad girlfriend or something.'

Ned frowned. 'I can understand the driving bit but I've never had a problem with the way you dress. Ever.'

Ivy reached out to him and took his hands. 'I know you haven't. That's what I mean. It's silly. It isn't even worth talking about. So let's not. Let's just forget what Jamie said and have our picnic.'

Ned held her gaze for several seconds.

'Then why did he say it? There's no smoke without fire, Ivy.'

'Ned! What *is* wrong with you? Since when do you care what anyone says? And I can assure you, there's not even smoke, let alone a fire. It's nonsense. Nothing but silly people saying silly things. Please, Ned. Let's not waste our time worrying about others. Let's just think of us.'

'I do think of us, Ivy. I think of us all the time. Perhaps that's half the problem. But you're right. I've only got an hour. We shouldn't waste it. We've hardly seen each other since Easter. Well, since you got your big promotion really.'

Was he blaming her for that? Was he saying that was her fault too? She was about to ask him but thought better of it. They'd already wasted too much time on words; what they both needed was some action. And preferably, a lot of it.

She let go of his hands, threw off her jacket and pulled her sweater over her head.

'Then let's go and see a lot of each other right now.'

Finally. The serious look on Ned's face was replaced with one much more to Ivy's liking.

Chapter Thirteen

Laurel loved The Coffee Hideaway. She loved being her own boss. She loved living above her business. She didn't even mind the long hours and the hard graft. She didn't particularly like doing admin and she positively loathed bookkeeping but apart from that, she loved her life. Well, not quite as much since realising she would never share it with Ned, but being single didn't worry her and she was glad that he was happy. There wasn't really anything about her life that she would change.

Except perhaps, to eat less cake. And possibly to drink less wine. The only other thing she would quite like, would be to have some time off. Especially on days like this when the May Day Market was in full swing and the crowning of the May Queen was taking place, followed by the May Queen's Parade. She used to love watching the entire ceremony. She even liked the Morris dancers… to a degree.

At least she could see the May Queen's Parade from her café. It passed right by the window, slowly snaking up Market Street from the makeshift stage in Market Field, turning around the war memorial outside St Catherine's Church before winding its way through five other streets in the village, finally returning to Market Field.

The café was virtually empty now, most of the customers having made their way outside to watch the parade. Only two remained; teenagers who no doubt considered themselves far too hip to watch such a spectacle, their heads down, their eyes glued to their smart phones.

Laurel locked the till. It wasn't that she didn't trust them but her mother had instilled in her the adage that it was better to be safe than sorry. She dropped the keys in her apron pocket and walked to the window, slipping off her shoes to stand on one of the red and white check cushioned chairs. It would give her a better view over the heads of the cheering spectators already crowding the pavement.

The parade wasn't far away. The rhythmic beats of the Hideaway Down Drummers were getting closer by the second, stirring up some deep-set primal instinct and making her want to dance. Not a sensible move when standing on a chair, and she pressed her fingers against the window pane to steady herself when the café door opened.

Oh no. What was he doing back here?

'Hi. May I join you?' Jamie grabbed a chair, placed it close to Laurel's and slipped off his shoes.

'Would it make any difference if I said no?'

He grinned. 'No.' He stepped up onto the seat and peered through the glass. 'Your windows need cleaning.'

Laurel gasped. 'Is there anything you like about this place?'

He turned to face her and his grin grew even more mischievous. 'Yes. There's one thing I like a lot.'

Her face burned under his scrutiny but there was no way she was going to let him get the better of her.

'It must be my coffee in spite of what you said earlier. This is the third time you've been here today.'

'No, Laurel. It's not your coffee.'

She coughed and fixed her gaze on the street. 'Do they

celebrate May Day like this where you come from?'

His laugh was a far happier sound than she'd expected.

'Where I come from? That would be Surrey, Laurel. I'm English, remember. But yes, I think they have a May Day parade in L.A. I don't think it's like this though. I've never been to it, so I couldn't say for sure. I hear the May Queen has a ring through her nose.'

'She's still beautiful.'

'I'm sure she is. I expect you were the May Queen once. I bet you were stunning.'

'I think every girl in this village has been, or will be, the May Queen. There're only so many females of an appropriate age at any given time and the village doesn't like to leave anyone out. And no, I wasn't stunning. I was sixteen and unfortunately going through a spotty phase. Holly and Ivy tried to cover both my spots and freckles with about a tonne of make-up. Mum said that I looked as if my face had been pebble-dashed.'

'Is your mum always so... delightful?'

Laurel met his look. 'Yes. She doesn't mean to be... mean. And honestly, she doesn't realise that her words hurt sometimes. I'm used to it though and in a funny way, she thinks she's being kind. That she's saying things for my own good. My brother, Graydon was always telling her off about it but she just couldn't see it. She still can't. And I *really* have no idea why I'm telling you this. Let's change the subject.'

'Okay. One final question. Does she do the same to Graydon?'

'No. Graydon's her golden boy. He nearly died when he was very young and I think Mum's taken special care of him ever since.' Laurel glanced at Jamie and grinned. 'Which is one of the reasons why Graydon's a barista in New York and not co-owner of The Coffee Hideaway.'

Jamie returned her smile. 'I understand *that* completely. My mum still wanted to accompany me to auditions when I was eighteen. She's one of the reasons I moved to L.A.'

They grinned at one another until a loud burst from a horn announced the arrival of the May Queen Parade.

'Are they... geese, leading the parade?' The surprise was evident in Jamie's voice.

'That's the Gaggle Gang. They run this village and no one gets in their way. Every procession, parade or event features the Gaggle Gang. They live in a woodshed at Meg Stanbridge's and they're Hideaway Down's pride and joy.'

'They must be very tame to wear those floral crowns, and all those colourful ribbons.'

'They're always dressed for the occasion, no matter what. They'll even make an appearance at the May Dance tonight, although one turn around the room is usually enough for them. They'll follow Meg home by eight-thirty, for their treats and an early night.'

'Gabriel mentioned the dance. Are you going with anyone?'

'We'll all be going. We always do. Everyone in the village goes.'

Jamie cleared his throat. 'So I hear. But are you going *with* anyone?'

Laurel studied his profile. 'As in "a date", you mean?'

'Yes.' He didn't look at her.

'No.'

'Will you go with me?' He still didn't look at her.

'Are you... Are you asking me on a date?'

'Would you say yes if I were?'

'No.' She couldn't suppress a giggle.

'Then I'm not. What time do you finish here?'

'I close at six.'

'Great. I'll pick you up at seven-thirty and we'll have dinner in the pub.'

'Jamie! I'm not going on a date with you.'

'Of course you're not.'

Now he did look at her – and her knees wobbled. She was sure of it.

'But… You just said you'd pick me up at seven-thirty and we'll have dinner in the pub!'

'Yes. With Holly and Gabriel, and Ivy and Ned.' He looked away. 'Here comes the float with the May Queen on. You're right. She is beautiful. And that ring is hardly visible from here.'

Chapter Fourteen

Laurel twisted and turned in front of her full-length mirror, sighed and discarded yet another outfit to the ever-growing pile of crumpled clothes on her bed. What was the matter with her? It was only the May Dance she was going to, not a ball, and the May Queen was hardly Elizabeth II. Having dinner in The Snowdrop Inn wasn't like having dinner in a posh restaurant. She didn't need to make too much of an effort. She didn't need to dress up. She never dressed up – well, perhaps once in a blue moon but her style was definitely 'casual'. She had dresses but not 'dressy' ones. She rarely wore make-up and she couldn't remember the last time she'd done anything with her poker-straight hair other than merely blow dry it or tie it in a ponytail.

So why was she taking so much trouble tonight? She'd spent close to half an hour slathering fake tan on her legs so that she wouldn't have to wear tights, and then a further thirty minutes doing her make-up and tonging her hair into large, loose waves. Her skin looked like porcelain and her freckles were barely visible so at least it had been worth the time and attention.

She glanced at her watch. Oh God, it was seven-fifteen. He would be here in fifteen minutes. No. *They* would be here, not just *him*. This wasn't a date. This. Was. Not. A. Date. She must remember that.

She spotted the dress she had bought for New Year's Eve; the dress she had bought specifically to impress Ned. It was during a shopping trip to Eastbourne in the first week of December and the moment she saw it she knew that if any dress had the ability to make her look good, it was that one even though it was the type of dress she would never normally dream of wearing. It seemed to call her name. From the second she tried it on, it gave her confidence; confidence perhaps to finally tell Ned how she felt as the clock struck midnight on the last night of the year. The dress she had never worn. Because Ned had started dating Ivy just before Christmas and the dress, along with all its promises of a bright new future, had been consigned to the back of her wardrobe where it had hung ever since in its plastic shroud.

It was as if the dress possessed some magical properties; she tingled as she pulled it out. Actually tingled. It sparkled as she held it up beneath the pint-sized, imitation chandelier hanging from her bedroom ceiling, the crystal droplets picking out several of the minute heart-shaped diamantes sprinkled like stars across the midnight-blue bodice. The gossamer skirt shimmered over its ivory petticoat, giving the entire dress an impression of fluidity.

Was it too much for the May Dance? Would she look as if she were trying too hard? In previous years, many of the villagers had really gone to town with their outfits. Why not her? What would her mother say?

She ran her hand over the material. Who cared what her mother said! Wasn't she always telling her to take a chance? To show people what Laurel French was really made of. But what if Holly and Ivy didn't dress up? Did she really want to be the odd one out? To stand out in the crowd? She held the dress against her and smiled. Yes. Yes, she did. She slipped it off the hanger, tossed the hanger on the pile and slid the dress over her tong-curled ginger-brown hair.

It was tighter than when she'd bought it but thankfully the material had some give in it. Unfortunately, that resulted in it being even more tightly fitting, especially around her bust. Four months of comfort eating had added at the very least, an inch, possibly two. She was definitely showing people what Laurel French was made of, wearing this.

The doorbell chimes rang out. Was it seven-thirty already? No time to change now. In three gulps, she emptied the large glass of wine she'd been drinking, put on her midnight-blue sandals and grabbed the matching clutch bag, her heart beating louder than the Hideaway Down Drummers in the May Queen Parade. She almost forgot the imitation sapphire and diamond earrings she'd left on her dressing table but remembered seconds before dashing down the stairs leading to the main front door at the side of the coffee shop.

'Wow!' Jamie's eyes raked over her body as she stood in the doorway. 'You look sensational.'

That was probably his usual line but she didn't care. It was good to hear someone say it to her.

'Thank you. You don't look bad yourself.' He didn't. In fact, he looked pretty darned hot in his black casual trousers and a light blue shirt beneath his leather jacket. Laurel gave herself a shake. 'Your bruise almost matches my dress. Does that hurt?'

Jamie grinned. 'You *almost* sound as if you care.'

'I *almost* do. I don't like to see anyone get hurt. But sometimes karma's a bitch.'

He burst out laughing. 'Just karma, Laurel? You know something? The more I see of you, the more I like you... especially in that dress. Did you buy it for someone special? He's a very lucky man.'

How did he know that? How could he possibly know

that?

'It's just a dress. I liked it. I bought it. No man involved.'

Jamie shook his head as his eyes travelled the length of her body once again.

'No, Laurel. That is definitely *not* "just a dress". That's a lethal weapon and it has the power to make men lose all reason. Believe me. I'm an expert when it comes to seduction.'

'Now that I do believe.' Dragging her eyes from his appreciative face, she glanced up and down Market Street. 'Um. Where're the others?'

'Ah. I've got a little confession to make. Now don't bite my head off. We're meeting them later.'

'We're what?'

'Don't look so horrified. It's not the end of the world, Laurel.'

'That's your opinion. You said this wasn't a date. I told you I wouldn't go on a date with you.'

'Yeah, you did. But would it be so bad? I mean, I'm not revolting, am I?'

She slowly scanned his body, trying to compose herself. 'I've been out with worse. But only by a margin. I don't like playing games, Jamie. I'm not good at it.'

'It? Are we talking about sex now?'

'What? No! No one's talking about sex.'

He grinned. 'Can we?'

'Can we... can we what? No, don't answer that. I don't want to know. This is a mistake. This is *not* happening.'

She turned to go back inside but he grabbed her hand, sending ripples through her body.

'Don't go. I'm sorry. If I promise not to behave like a jerk, will you have dinner with me? Please will you have dinner with me? Come on, Laurel. You've got to eat. It's just food and wine. You like food and wine, don't you?'

Laurel caught her breath. 'I think that's abundantly clear. I think I like food and wine a bit too much, and it's starting to show. Far more than I'd like, if I'm honest.'

Again, those eyes. Again, that strange sensation. What was happening to her? And had she really just told him that she thought she was fat? What is wrong with you, woman?

'As I said when you opened the door, you look sensational. Come on, Laurel. Let me take the prettiest woman in the village to dinner.'

'I think Ivy's busy.'

'Don't do that.' He sounded cross. 'Don't put yourself down.'

'I…' She couldn't think of anything to say.

'You're in love with Ned, aren't you?'

'What!' She must be having a heart attack. Her heart was racing; her ears were ringing; her breath coming in short sharp gasps. Or a panic attack. 'No. I… Of course not. I… I don't feel well.'

He slid an arm around her waist. Now she really felt strange. She took several deep breaths; aware that he was watching her. Reading every action.

'Are you okay? I'm sorry. I shouldn't have come right out and said it like that. It's true though, isn't it? Don't worry. Your secret's safe with me. I promise you I won't say a word. I may be many things, Laurel, but I'm not all bad. You can trust me on this.'

'How… How did you know?'

'I'm an actor. I study people for a living. I notice the way they look at things. Their gestures. Their eyes. The way they breathe. The way they move. I can't help it. It's automatic. Almost like I'm programmed to do it. And I saw the way you looked at Ned this morning. The way you peered around me to watch him walk down the street. I saw the expression on your face and the love in your eyes.'

Laurel swallowed but a strangled laugh escaped. 'And there was me thinking you were studying the menu.'

Jamie laughed. 'You call *that* a menu.' He nudged her with his body, his arms still wrapped around her. 'I was. I can take in several things at once. I'm a superstar, remember. I have superpowers. And right now, I'm going to use my superpower to persuade you to have dinner with me. And another thing. To show that you can trust me with your secret, I'll tell you mine. I think I may have fallen for Ivy Gilroy. Let's go and drown our sorrows together.'

'You've fallen for Ivy!' Laurel moved herself away from Jamie's arm. 'Bloody hell, Jamie. You only met her today.'

'It only takes a moment to fall in love, Laurel.' He winked. 'I've done it hundreds of times in movies.'

Laurel tutted. 'Do you take anything seriously? What you really mean is, you're lusting after her. Well, join the queue with the others.'

He tipped his head to one side. 'Gabriel didn't. From what I hear Ivy wasn't dating Ned when Gabriel arrived. He could have chosen Ivy or Holly. He fell in love with Holly. And that helps prove my point. Gabriel fell in love with Holly the moment he met her.' He laughed suddenly. 'He told me that she came to the door wearing reindeer-patterned pyjamas, her hair piled up on her head like a ramshackle birds nest wrapped in Christmas ribbon and tied with a bow. And that she had a ring of toothpaste around her mouth. If that doesn't prove love is not only blind, but strikes at the strangest moment, nothing will.'

Laurel giggled. 'I remember Holly telling me how

embarrassed she felt about that. Did Gabriel really tell you that was when he fell in love with her?'

'Uh-huh.' Jamie nodded. 'Although he didn't realise it was love at the time. He simply couldn't believe that he'd got the hots for a woman who looked completely mad but somehow beautiful.'

'Holly *is* beautiful. Both she and Ivy look good no matter what they wear or how they dress. If that had been me standing on the doorstep, I'd have just looked completely mad.'

'No, Laurel. No, you wouldn't. You'd have looked completely beautiful. But not as beautiful as you do tonight.'

'I don't get you. You've been flirting with me since virtually the moment you arrived. You've just told me you've fallen for Ivy and now you're flirting with me again, even though you've also just told me that you know I'm in love with Ned. Are you always like this? Always so…'

'So... what?'

'It doesn't matter.'

'So... what, Laurel?'

'So shallow.'

He held her gaze. 'Yes. Yes I think I am. But I also think Ivy could change me. Don't look at me like that. I'm serious. In fact I think she already has changed me. I feel like a different man from the one who arrived this morning. And it isn't just the jetlag. I really do feel different.'

'Perhaps that bruise on your jaw has something to do with it. Perhaps you're suffering from some form of concussion.'

He shook his head. 'It's not concussion. Something's happened to me, that's for sure. Perhaps it was your coffee.'

Laurel grinned. 'I might've guessed my coffee would be to blame.'

'Is that you, Laurel?' Bartram Battersfold's voice broke in on their silent gaze like a cannonball. 'It is, isn't it? I hardly recognised you. You look… completely different.'

Petunia Welsley tutted; her arm linked through Bartram's, she pulled him close. 'What my darling man means, Laurel, is that you look absolutely beautiful. We spotted you the moment we left Bartram's and the nearer we got, the more beautiful you became. You really do look lovely, doesn't she, darling?'

'Didn't I just say that, darling? I'm sure I did. I meant to. You look beautiful, Laurel. Beautiful.'

Laurel's cheeks burned. 'Thank you. I… I thought it was about time I made an effort.'

Petunia smiled. 'I doubt that it took much effort, Laurel. I've always thought you were beautiful. You simply need to believe it. And who's this lucky young man? Ah, you must be the famous, Jamie McDay. Everyone in the village is talking about you.'

'Not just the village, from what I hear,' Bartram added. 'I suppose that's the trouble with being famous. Always in the spotlight. Everything you do. No place to hide. Is that why you've come to Hideaway Down? To try and hide?'

'Originally, yes.'

'Sorry. Where're my manners? Jamie, this is Petunia Welsley. Petunia owns Petunia's Perfumery, that heavenly shop just across the road and a few doors up.' Laurel pointed towards the shop. 'And this is Bartram Battersfold. Bartram is the village butcher. That's his shop a few doors away on this side of the road, just past The General Store and the cobbled alley leading to the car park.'

'Hi,' Jamie said, smiling and holding out his hand.

Bartram gave it a firm shake. Petunia gave it her usual, gentle touch.

'But not now?' Petunia asked, cocking her head to one side. 'You said that was why you originally came here. It's not the reason you're planning to stay?'

Laurel wasn't sure she liked the way Petunia glanced at her when she said that. If only Petunia knew what Jamie had just told her. That he had fallen for Ivy in a big, big way. What would Petunia have said then?

Jamie's smile widened. 'Let's just say, it's no longer the only reason.'

Petunia nodded and once again glanced at Laurel knowingly.

How wrong could someone be?

Jamie took Laurel's hand and linked it through his arm. 'We're going to The Snowdrop Inn for dinner and then the May Dance. To dance, I guess.'

'You're in for a treat,' Bartram said, his wide smile puffing out already puffy, red cheeks.

'Oh, I'm sure I am. One way or another. Are you headed in that direction?'

Petunia smiled. 'No. We are having dinner at the pub tonight, too, but we're popping in to my shop beforehand. We simply had to come and say hello, first. I hope you booked ahead. It's bound to be packed in there.'

Jamie returned the smile. 'I did. I booked it at lunchtime. Janet very kindly squeezed us in. After you.'

He stepped aside to let Petunia and Bartram pass, the pavement being too narrow for all four of them to walk side by side but Petunia pointed across the road towards her shop.

'We're going that way. See you later. Have fun.'

'And you.'

'You did what?' Laurel waved with her free hand and tugged at her arm but Jamie held it tight.

'Shush, Laurel. We don't want to spoil the impression Petunia and Bartram have of us.'

Laurel lowered her voice. 'You were pretty sure of yourself, weren't you? You booked it before you even asked me. Did you tell Janet you would be bringing me? You didn't say it was a date, did you?'

'Oddly enough, I wasn't sure of myself but yes, I did book it before I'd asked you. Yes, I did tell Janet I would be bringing you and I think she assumed it was on a date but I'm not sure I told her that.'

'Well, you can let go of my hand now. They've gone, and I'm perfectly capable of walking down the street, thank you very much.'

'I'm sure you are. I'm sure you're capable of a lot of things. But I like holding your hand, Laurel. It feels… reassuring somehow.'

Reassuring wasn't the word she would use. It didn't feel in the least bit reassuring to her. Anything but reassuring, in fact. And yet the strange thing was, she rather liked him holding her hand, too. Like the dress she was wearing, it made her feel confident enough to face the world. Even confident enough to face seeing Ned and Ivy together without feeling somehow inferior or inadequate – and that was nothing short of amazing.

Chapter Fifteen

The Snowdrop Inn was bursting at the seams. Customers spilled out over the grassy bank, mingling with the Morris dancers and the May Queen, who looked exquisite in her pink gown and her attendants dressed in white. Even the Gaggle Gang, still wearing their crowns and ribbons sat huddled beneath the blossoming chestnut tree, their orange bills and bright blue eyes pointed towards a wild-haired woman, also dressed in white. She sat perched on a chair in front of them, her cherubic face the colour of cherries and the soft golden rays of the setting sun cast her in a pale, warm spotlight.

Jamie smiled. 'Who's that? She looks as though she's telling the geese a story.'

Laurel laughed. 'That's Meg Stanbridge. Remember I said the Gaggle Gang live in her woodshed? The truth is, she idolises them. Treats them like children. And they in return, behave like naughty teenagers. One of them is always disappearing, resulting in the entire village forming a search party to find it. But I suppose the plain fact is, we're all as much in love with them as Meg.'

'And no one's ever tried to grab one for Sunday lunch.'

'No one would dare. Hanging may be banned in this country, but believe me, if anyone so much as laid a finger on one of those geese, the entire village would help with the lynching. And that includes me.'

'Just as well I'm a vegetarian then.'

'Are you? That surprises me.'

'Sorry. No, I'm not. It was a joke. A poor one,

obviously. Better not give up the day job. Although it may have given me up.'

'Is that a joke too? Is there really a chance you'll be dropped from the next film?'

'It's no joke. And yes, there's a very good chance. I've only got myself to blame. I could've just dumped Perdita and walked away. Better still, I could've dumped her in private and not made a complete idiot of myself in front of anyone who's anyone in the film industry.'

'Is that what happened? You dumped your girlfriend in public? Why did you hit the guy? Oh, was there something going on between them?'

'Yes. The stupid thing is, I didn't love Perdita. We only started dating to gain publicity for ourselves, and for the first film. It sort of carried on from there. We had a fairly open relationship in reality. The problem was I couldn't stand that guy. If it had been anyone else, it wouldn't have mattered. But when I heard that he was bragging that Perdita preferred him to me, I kinda lost it. God knows why. I should've simply said: 'You're welcome to her, pal.' But I didn't. And drink makes me behave like an even bigger idiot than I already am.'

'Drink has the same effect on me. It's the devil's drug.' Laurel grinned as Jamie held open the pub door and the bells tinkled overhead.

'Is that what the local vicar says? Or your mum?'

'Neither. It's what the old vicar used to say. That and a lot more besides.'

'Hell, it's crowded in here. Shall I go first?'

Laurel grinned at him. 'What, and forge a path?'

'Something like that. Here, take my hand.'

'I can manage to make my own way to the bar without your assistance, thanks very much.'

'Fine. You were saying about the vicar?'

'That's it really. Ivy used to call him Vile Vincent but since our new vicar arrived and started wearing T-shirts with Kev the Rev emblazoned across the front, Ivy changed the previous one to Vincent the Venomous Vicar. He was loathsome. The church nearly went into decline. If there was ever a man to make the devil look like the lesser of two evils, it was Vincent.'

'That was the original name for my character in the vampire films but it was decided that Adam was better.'

'Is he evil? Or is he some sort of semi tragic-romantic figure?'

'Adam's very romantic. And tragic. And very funny in a sarcastic slash horrific way. I'll have to take you to see the films. Or we could hire them on DVD. The first two are out but the third film won't be released to the big screen until later this year. D'you fancy that? A night in with me and my vampire alter-ego? Or d'you want to see how this date goes first?'

'This is not a date, Jamie. As for a night in with you and your alter-ego, I think I'd rather wash my hair. No offence. I like my hair.'

That made him laugh. 'None taken. I like your hair too. Perhaps I could help you wash it.' He finally made it to the bar and waved at Janet.'

'Laurel!' Janet sounded as astonished as she looked. 'Gosh, Laurel, you look gorgeous. I love that dress. It really suits you. I don't think I've ever seen you look so stunning. You'll be turning heads in here tonight, you can bet on that.'

Laurel's cheeks flushed crimson and she lowered her head a fraction. 'Thanks, Janet. I... I bought it before Christmas. I thought it was about time I wore it.'

'Well I hope this young man told you how positively breathtaking you look.'

'I did. More than once, I believe. It's busy in here.'

'Maybe they've heard we've got a movie star in town. Oh, don't look so worried. It's always busy in here. Especially when there's something going on, like this May Day weekend.'

'Did someone say "movie star"?' A man in his late fifties with bushy ginger hair swivelled round on his barstool, eyed Jamie up and down and beamed at him. 'So this is what a movie star looks like, is it? Could've fooled me. You could do with some sun on your bones, lad. I hear you're a friend of Gabriel's. Hope you've got a better sense of direction than that lad has. I'm Henry. Henry Goode. Pleased to meet you. You can buy an old farmer a pint if you like. I hear you're made of money. Got several million dollars for getting in and out of a coffin, so I'm told. That true? Perhaps I should send my son Harry over to Hollywood. He's a good-looking lad.'

Laurel laughed and kissed Henry on the cheek. 'Henry, this is Jamie. Jamie meet Henry. He owns Hideaway Farm. You can see it from Holly Cottage.'

'Good to meet you, Henry.' Jamie held out his hand and Henry beamed at him for a second time. 'You've got an ultra-friendly smile.'

'New teeth.' Henry tapped his two upper front teeth with his finger. 'Got 'em for Christmas. Lost the originals when I took a tumble from my tractor. Solid as a rock these are. Titanium posts, they tell me. Seems titanium costs more than gold. Told the wife I'll buy her a titanium necklace come our next anniversary. Pity I didn't save my original teeth. Could've strung them on it.' He beamed again, reaching up and slapping Jamie on the shoulder.

'Where *is* Beth?' Laurel glanced around the crowded pub.

'Powdering her nose, so she said. Catching up on

gossip more like. She'll be back shortly.'

'What can I get you?' Janet asked.

Jamie touched Laurel's arm. 'Laurel, what would you like?'

'A glass of red wine, please.'

He turned back to Janet. 'One red wine. A pint for me, please and a pint of whatever Henry's drinking. Plus whatever his wife drinks.'

'So you're on a date then, Laurel?' Henry winked at her and squeezed her arm. 'You best watch this lad. You know what these Hollywood types are like.'

Laurel sighed. 'It's not a date, Henry. And no, I don't know what they're like, but I am a quick learner.'

'Going to the dance?' Henry looked Laurel up and down. 'You'll be the belle of the ball in that dress. Has Trixie seen you yet?'

Laurel sighed again. 'Not yet, Henry. She's here, I take it?'

'Yep. And I suspect my Beth isn't far away from her.'

Laurel looked around her and leant close to Jamie, placing a hand on his shoulder and easing his head towards her, her soft breath only inches from his ear.

'I'd better get it over with. Excuse me for a moment. If I don't go and say hello now, Mum will find us later, and as much as I love her, that's an experience we could both do without.'

He turned his head to face her as the tinkling bells over the pub door announced its opening, but the shiver that ran through him when his eyes met hers wasn't caused by the draught from the open door.

This could be a problem. In Hollywood, it wouldn't matter. You could date two women at the same time and no one would bat an eye. Hell, you could even sleep with two women at the same time – literally – and no one

112

would give it a second thought. Threesomes weren't an issue... unless the paparazzi found out. But in Hideaway Down, such behaviour would be tantamount to murder. He was pretty sure of that.

What was he to do? He thought Laurel was attractive when he saw her first thing this morning but the minute he saw Ivy, he was blown away. He hadn't felt like that in a long time.

But now this evening, seeing Laurel look like this and getting to know her... something was happening – he simply wasn't sure what. And he wasn't sure he liked it. Could he really have fallen for two different women, both of whom were in love with the same man? A man so completely opposite to him in nearly every way possible.

And that wasn't the worst of it. Usually, when he met women, it was all about their looks... and all about getting them into bed. Sometimes relationships developed from there. Sometimes they didn't. One-night stands weren't an issue in Hollywood either, provided you were careful and made sure you used protection. But it was different with these women. He wasn't just attracted by their looks; he was attracted by their personalities. This was definitely a first for him.

He watched Laurel edge her way through the crowd to find her mother and suddenly, he wanted to protect her. To build up her confidence instead of knocking it down as he suspected Trixie did, whether meaning to or not. It was clear Laurel felt somehow inferior to Ivy, and to Holly for that matter, and yet she had no cause to. Not only was she pretty; she had her own business too. And people liked her; that much was obvious.

What was he to do? He wanted Ivy more than he'd wanted anyone for a long, long time, but when Laurel placed her hand on his shoulder and whispered in his ear, he had struggled to resist the urge to pull her into his arms and kiss her. Yes. This was a new experience for him and he had no idea how he would handle it. Laurel had said it earlier: "Sometimes karma is a bitch."

Henry tapped Jamie's shoulder as Janet placed two pints on the bar.

'Not a date, eh?' Henry beamed at him, raising one of the pints in a toast. 'Here's to love and all its complications.'

Jamie studied Henry's face. Had Henry Goode just read his mind?

Chapter Sixteen

Laurel could not believe she was having so much fun. Nor could she believe how many compliments she was getting. First, Petunia and Bartram. Well, strictly speaking, Jamie was first. He didn't count though. He probably said stuff like that to all the girls. Petunia and Bartram were genuine. She knew them well enough to realise that. Then there was Henry – although he always said every woman in the village looked lovely even on their worst hair day, their nose running, and dressed like a bundle of rags. Several others had paid her compliments and she could tell by their eyes that they were sincerely meant. But her mother's reaction surprised her the most. Trixie actually stopped mid-conversation with Beth, her mouth fell open, her eyes grew as large as saucers and a single tear ran down her rouged cheek.

'Laurel!'

Laurel waited for the put-down but it didn't come. Instead, Trixie got up from her chair and took both of Laurel's hands in hers, stretching their arms wide, in order to get a better look at Laurel's dress.

'My goodness me. I never thought I'd see the day. The ugly duckling turns into a swan. Not that I'm saying you're ugly. Far from it. You've got an interesting face. I've always said so. But this…' Trixie scanned Laurel from head to foot. 'Well this, my darling girl is every mother's dream. To see her daughter's inner beauty shine through like this. Pass me my phone, Beth. I must take a photo. Better still, will you take a photo of me and my beautiful daughter together? I want to send it to Graydon's Facebook page.'

For a moment, Laurel had been tempted to ask where her real mother was, and could the aliens please bring her back? But she resisted the urge because she didn't want to spoil the moment and she was in no hurry for her real mum to return. Instead, Laurel posed for several pictures, all the while thinking this was a really magical dress. If she had known a dress had this much power, she would have searched the world to find one long before now.

'I've got to go, Mum. I'm here with someone.'

'Someone? A man?' Trixie's eyes lit up even more; if that were possible. 'Are you on a date?'

Laurel hesitated for a split second. 'Yes, Mum. With Jamie McDay. The man from my café this morning.'

'The Hollywood movie star?'

Laurel nodded. 'Yes. We're having dinner here and then we're going to the May Dance.'

'Well then, don't keep him waiting, my girl. You go and have some fun. But I want to hear all about it first thing tomorrow. Can you believe it, Beth? My beautiful daughter dating a Hollywood movie star!'

Beth Goode nodded and smiled. 'I can easily believe it. Laurel's a rare bloom. Even Henry says so. Have a wonderful evening, Laurel dear.'

Laurel gave a quick wave and a broad smile. If she stayed any longer she might shed a tear herself and that would ruin her make-up. She walked back to Jamie with an air of confidence, much greater than she had ever experienced before, and the strangest feeling that something even more miraculous was going to happen.

Chapter Seventeen

Jamie was enjoying himself. If anyone had told him a week ago that having dinner with an ordinary woman, in an ordinary, English village pub, discussing May Day festivities and a dance in a church hall, would give him so much pleasure, he would have had them certified.

But the reality was The Snowdrop Inn was not an ordinary village pub, and Hideaway Down was not an ordinary English village from what little of it he had seen so far. And Laurel French was definitely not an ordinary woman. She was kind; she was loyal; she was amusing in the very best way; she was a good listener; she even gave good advice and there was absolutely no question about it: she was beautiful, both inside and out.

It was dark outside by the time Jamie and Laurel left the pub, and when Jamie looked up, the cloudless, night sky was filled with stars. The village didn't have much in the way of street lights so it was just as well that a half-full moon cast a silvery glow on the road ahead of them as they strolled up Market Street side by side. He considered taking her hand but resisted the temptation. She was telling him more about the village and its residents and it was clear how much she loved the place. It was also clear how much she loved Ned Stelling.

'That's Ned's smithy.' She pointed to a large stable door, illuminated by the street lamp right outside. 'And that's his ironmonger's shop next door. His mum, Audrey used to man the till there but she's been rather poorly since the start of this year, so Ned's locked the shop door and now sells directly from his smithy via a connecting door inside.'

'Is that his place too?' Jamie pointed to the tiny shop the other side of the smithy, its window overflowing with baskets which, even in the shadows, Jamie could tell were handmade.

'No. Those are traditional Sussex trugs. That takes a completely different set of skills. Violet Day owns that. She's been weaving baskets there for longer than most people can remember. She's eighty-four next week. Ned often helps her out with lifting the bales of chestnut and willow she uses to make the trugs.'

'Sounds like Ned's a busy man.'

'He is. But he always manages to find time to help other people. That's one of the things I love about... I mean... He's very kind.' Laurel lowered her eyes and her cheeks flushed a soft shade of red.

Jamie glanced back at Ned's smithy as they walked on. Ned Stelling was an exceedingly lucky man. He was lucky to have Ivy and he didn't even know how lucky he was that a woman such as Laurel was in love with him.

'How long have you been in love with Ned, Laurel?'

'What? Um. Can we please not start that again? I really don't want to talk about it. There's simply no point. He's with Ivy now and it's apparent how much he loves her. Ah, this is Holly's bookshop. Well, it will be when she and Gabriel have cleaned and decorated it.'

Jamie peered through the grimy windows into the darkness of the double fronted shop.

'It's not very big. Is there much call for a bookshop in a village like this? I thought bookshops were closing down. Is it wise to be opening one, especially in such a remote place? She's not doing this because Gabriel's an author, is she?'

'No! Holly loves books. She used to run a bookshop in Eastbourne… until it closed down and she was made redundant.'

'Hmm. My point exactly. So having seen a bookshop in a large town go under, she decides to open a tiny bookshop in a small village. I say again, is that wise? I'm surprised Gabriel hasn't talked her out of it.'

'It's Holly's dream. It always has been. She knows there's a chance it might not work but the thing about this village is, people come from miles around to visit it, and its shops. They buy things here that they might not buy in a large town. Holly plans to sell mainly older books, as in the rare or antique ones, and more commonplace, second-hand ones with old-fashioned bindings. And Gabriel's all for it. Especially as Holly also intends to have a dedicated 'romance' section where she will also stock modern and new books, including all Gabriella Mann's novels.'

Jamie smiled. 'I can see Gabriel being in favour of that.'

'Ivy suggested that Holly should start a dating business as a sideline and call it Book Lovers, or something. It would be for people who're passionate about books, to come and meet like-minded, potential partners. She even said that perhaps I could stay open late on those evenings so that, having met a person they liked the look of, the 'new' couple could go for coffee at my place, or for a drink at the pub.'

'That's not such a crazy idea. Is Holly doing it?'

Laurel laughed and shook her head. 'I think she needs to get the bookshop up and running first. She can think about that at a later time. Starting one business is a big risk. There's no point in taking an even bigger risk by starting two.'

'Sometimes we have to take several risks to get what

we really want.'

'What she really wants is a bookshop.'

'What about you, Laurel?' Jamie reached out and took her hand. 'What do you really want?'

Because he had stopped, Laurel had to stop too. She looked uneasy and wouldn't meet his eyes. 'I've got everything I want.'

'Seriously? Everything?'

Now she looked cross. 'Jamie. Please don't keep going on about this. There are some things in life we simply can't have. We have to deal with it and move on.'

'But you haven't moved on, have you? Ned started dating Ivy four months ago and yet you're still in love with him.'

Laurel blinked several times and took a long, steady breath. 'I'm trying hard not to be. Unfortunately, it's taking longer than I expected to get over him.'

'What if you didn't have to get over him? What if, deep down, he felt the same way about you?'

Laurel blinked faster. 'Don't be ridiculous. He doesn't. He loves Ivy.'

'I agree. He does love Ivy. But I saw the way he looked at you this morning, Laurel and I'm telling you, Ned Stelling cares more about you than either he's willing to admit, or he doesn't even know he feels.'

She hesitated for a second. 'Nonsense. You've been in too many movies. This is real life, Jamie. Ned cares about me, I know he does, but as a friend. That's it. Nothing more.'

'I think you're wrong. And I think you need to show him how you feel about him.'

'Good God! You sound just like my mother. That's what she's always telling me to do.'

'I hate to say this, but I think she's right. Perhaps if

you'd listened to her sooner, you would be going to this dance with Ned. Then Ivy would have been free to go with me.'

Laurel's jaw dropped and her eyes widened. She yanked her hand free from his and glowered at him.

'Is that what this is really all about? Did you ask Ivy to dinner and the dance? Did she tell you she was going with Ned? Was I some sort of substitute?'

'No!'

'I don't believe you. Are you... are you playing some sort of game? You somehow realised I'm in love with Ned and you thought... I don't know what you thought. That there might be a slim chance that Ned would see me with you and suddenly decide he's been in love with me all along, or something equally ridiculous?'

'Why's that so ridiculous?'

Laurel gasped. 'So that was your plan? That's why you asked me?'

'No. Not exactly. I asked you because... because I like you. I like talking to you. But yes, it did occur to me that Ned might be jealous if he saw us together.'

'What? Jealous enough to dump Ivy so that you could comfort her. And then ask her out yourself? My God. You're not just shallow, you're a bastard!'

'I'm trying to help you out. Can't you see that? Don't you want Ned to be jealous? Wouldn't you like him to realise he's in love with you and dump Ivy?'

'No, Jamie. This may come as a surprise to you but I want Ned to be happy and if him being happy means that he's with someone else, then so be it.'

'Is he happy? From what I've heard, they're complete opposites and I've seen for myself that not everything's going well in their relationship. They've only been dating for a few months and there're already cracks appearing.

Don't you want to take advantage of those and finally get the man you want? The man you love?'

'I don't know what "cracks" you're talking about but I have no intention of using those – or anything else – to try to break up their relationship. Yes, I agree they're complete opposites but opposites attract. They love one another and that's all that matters.'

'Now it's you who's seen too many movies, Laurel. Opposites may attract but it takes a great deal more than attraction to make a relationship last a lifetime. It helps if people have things in common.'

'What would you know about it? From what I hear, your relationships rarely last a month, let alone a lifetime. You said yourself you weren't in love with your last girlfriend and that you had an open relationship, so don't pretend to know what makes a good relationship work because I doubt if you have the faintest idea.'

'I know what doesn't make it work. Two people wanting totally different things. Ned is firmly rooted in this village. Ivy's a free spirit. That's obvious to anyone with an iota of sense. Can you see her leaving London and spending her life above the blacksmith's shop? Because that's what she'll have to do if she stays with Ned. There's no way that man's going anywhere.'

'You've been in this village for one day. Just one day. How can you possible know so much about what you think people will and won't do?'

'Are you saying I'm wrong? Are you telling me that Ned would move to London if Ivy asked him to? Or that Ivy would settle into village life without once regretting what she's given up to be here?'

'Ivy doesn't have to give up anything. She could commute to London. It's not impossible.'

'With kids at home? Because I'm pretty certain Ned

Stelling is the kind of man who'll want a house full of kids sometime in the not too distant future. Or am I wrong about that, too? You may think I'm a bastard, Laurel and I agree I've only been here for one day but I'm telling you this... unless either Ivy or Ned is prepared to make a massive sacrifice to stay together, that relationship is ultimately doomed.'

'I…'

'You know I'm right, don't you?'

Her eyes narrowed but it was obvious her fight had gone.

'I don't know. There may be something in what you say.'

'Well, isn't it better if they find out sooner rather than later?'

'I'm not going to pretend to be with you in the hope of making Ned jealous, Jamie. I can assure you of that. And I'm not going to flirt with Ned, either. Ivy's my friend and I won't try to steal my friend's boyfriend. Ever.'

'I'm not asking you to.'

'Then what are you asking me to do?'

'Nothing. I'm simply telling you that I know how you feel about Ned and that there's a possibility he feels the same about you. That's it. And for your information, I didn't ask Ivy to dinner or the dance. I asked you. I'll admit I was hoping that you and I could work together and that way we could both get what we want but I realise now that was a mistake. That's fine. It doesn't mean I didn't enjoy having dinner with you and it doesn't mean I won't enjoy going to the dance with you.'

Laurel gave a peel of laughter. 'You want me to go to the dance with you after this? You really are unbelievable, Jamie McDay.'

'Why not? Didn't you enjoy yourself at dinner?'

'Y-e-s. Thank you.'

'And don't you think you'd enjoy yourself at the dance with me?'

Laurel tipped her head to one side. 'That, I'm not sure about.'

'Okay. Well then, wouldn't you prefer to go to the dance with me than to turn up on your own?'

She studied his face for what seemed like an eternity before shaking her head and letting out a sigh.

'Yes. I suppose I would. But I'm telling you now, there is no way on this earth that I am flirting with Ned, or trying to make him jealous in any way. Okay?'

'Okay. Are we friends again?'

'Again? I hadn't realised we were friends to start with.'

'Your mum was right. If that tongue of yours was any sharper, you'd cut yourself... my girl.' He winked at her and took her hand. 'Come on then. Show me what this May Dance is all about.'

She tried to pull her hand away but he held it tight and they walked the rest of the short distance to the church hall in silence.

Chapter Eighteen

Laurel couldn't think of anything else to say as she and Jamie walked, hand in hand, to the May Dance. The evening had taken a strange turn and her mind was racing from that bizarre and slightly heated conversation. Was there any truth in what he said? Were Ivy and Ned having problems? Was Jamie right about that? He was definitely wrong about Ned returning her own feelings. If Ned loved her at all, it was only as a friend.

'Is this it?' Jamie stopped in front of a large wooden sign with a floral-decorated poster declaring: 'May Dance. Here tonight. 8 till late'.

'This is it. St Catherine's Church Hall. Not much like the Hollywood events you're used to, I don't suppose.'

He grinned. 'Oh I don't know. It's certainly smaller but I've been to some pretty strange events.'

'I don't doubt it.'

'Laurel! Laurel, is that you?'

Laurel glanced over her shoulder. 'Hi, Holly. Hi, Gabriel. I thought you'd already be inside.'

'No. We only had supper about an hour ago. We were sorting out more paperwork for the bookshop and we were running late. You look fantastic! Doesn't she, Gabriel?'

'Absolutely.'

Gabriel looked at Jamie and immediately glanced down at their hands. Once again Laurel tugged her arm but Jamie held on tight and, as much as it irritated her, she didn't want to make a big thing of it. That would only create more questions and she could almost hear Gabriel's mind whirring already.

'Thanks. You look great too, Holly. That shade of red really suits you. I'm glad I'm not the only one who dressed up. I wasn't sure whether to or not.'

Holly smiled. 'When Jamie told us that he'd asked you on a date, I thought you might, so I did too. Ivy will as well.'

'Jamie told you…?' Laurel threw him a look but promptly fixed a smile in the hope that Holly wouldn't see how annoyed she was. 'Well, I suppose when a Hollywood movie star asks someone out, he expects them to make an effort.'

Jamie raised her hand to his lips and kissed it just as she spotted Ned and Ivy from the corner of her eye. Ivy looked stunning in a low-cut, dark green dress and Ned looked gorgeous as always. His chocolate-brown casual trousers were Laurel's favourites and the fawn short-sleeved shirt he was wearing showed off his tanned arms. Unlike the tan on Laurel's bare legs, Ned's wasn't fake. He had year-round colour from taking every opportunity to get out and about in the great outdoors and although Laurel did the same, she wore sunscreen of at least factor fifty.

Ivy wolf whistled; Ned seemed to be frowning.

'Bloody hell, Laurel! What's happened to you?' Ivy shrieked, followed by her cheery laughter. 'Sorry. That didn't come out right. What I meant was, you look incredible! Doesn't Laurel look incredible, Ned? I hardly recognised you.'

'That's what I said to Gabriel,' Holly added. 'In fact, I recognised Jamie before I recognised you, Laurel. You really do look amazing. You should dress like this more often.'

Ned didn't say a word.

Jamie let go of Laurel's hand and slid his arm around her waist, pulling her to him.

'Why does everyone sound so surprised that you look incredibly beautiful tonight? I could see how beautiful you were the moment I met you in The Coffee Hideaway this morning. Well, once Ned here had moved out of the way.' Jamie threw Ned a smile.

Ned didn't return the smile and Laurel could hardly breathe under the intensity of his gaze as his eyes scanned her from head to toe and back again.

'You're quiet, Ned.' Ivy nudged him in the side.

He glanced at her. 'Am I?'

Ivy frowned. 'Yes. And you're the only one who hasn't said how gorgeous Laurel looks. Have you gone blind or something?'

'Huh? Oh. Something like that. Laurel doesn't need me to tell her how incredible she looks. Besides, everyone else has said it.'

Jamie grinned. 'If you don't mind me saying, you've got a lot to learn about women, Ned. They never tire of being told they look beautiful.'

Ned glared at him. 'Laurel's not like that.'

'Excuse me! I'm standing right here you know. And actually, Ned, Jamie's right.' Laurel placed her hand on Jamie's shoulder. 'Women do like to be told. We all want to feel special.'

She hadn't meant to snap at him but that had annoyed her. He clearly didn't think she looked beautiful and that's why he couldn't say it. Jamie had been so wrong about him. Ned wasn't in the least bit attracted to her, that much was obvious.

'Of course we do.' Ivy playfully slapped Ned's arm. 'What's wrong with you? Can't you tell a friend how good she looks without getting grumpy?'

'I did tell her. And I'm not grumpy.'

Laurel stepped in. 'It doesn't matter, Ivy. If a compliment has to be forced, it's not really a compliment.' Now she forced a laugh. 'Come on. Let's go in. I want to dance.'

She slid her hand from Jamie's shoulder to his waist and arm in arm they went inside. As usual for the May Dance, the hall was decorated with row upon row of multi-coloured paper flowers, hung from beams and criss-crossing the entire ceiling. Potted trees stood in each corner strewn with brightly coloured ribbons and more paper flowers. To one side, there were trellis tables covered with dark green tablecloths on which stood bottles of various soft drinks, a few kegs of beer and three large glass bowls containing May Day Punch – a secret recipe known only to Janet Gilroy who supplied all of the beverages for the event. All the proceeds went to charity so Kev the Rev had no objection and neither did the local council as the appropriate licences were always easily obtained.

At the back of the hall, a DJ from Eastbourne, hired every year for the last five years, was playing a slow dance track and Laurel waved to him as she and Jamie walked through the double doors of the hall.

Jamie led her onto the dance floor, spinning her around in his arms before pulling her close in a tight embrace.

'I told you,' he whispered in her ear.

They were dancing cheek to cheek and as she tried to look at him, her lips brushed his jaw. She quickly leant away and struggled to find her voice.

'Told me what?'

'That Ned's nuts about you.'

She tutted. 'You're the one who's nuts. Everyone said how beautiful I looked except for Ned. Did you miss that?'

'Of course I didn't. And that's my point. He couldn't bring himself to say it.'

'Because he didn't think I looked beautiful.'

Jamie leant his head back and laughed. 'Oh, Laurel. You two are as bad as one another. You clearly deserve each other. The reason he couldn't say it wasn't because he didn't think it. It was because he suddenly realised just how beautiful you are and if he'd said that, he might not have been able to stop himself from saying something more.'

'What utter nonsense!'

'Believe what you want. You wait and see.' He pulled her closer and they danced in silence.

He was mistaken. He must be. Quivers of excitement ran through her. Was that because of Jamie's words? Because somewhere deep inside her she was hoping he was right. Or was it because he was holding her so close, she could feel the warmth of Jamie's body against hers?

She closed her eyes and rested her head on Jamie's shoulder, imagining for just a moment that it was Ned whose arms held her so tightly, and whose cheek lay softly against her hair... that it was Ned's aftershave that filled her nostrils and made her senses reel... Ned's voice she could hear.

She lifted her head abruptly. 'Sorry. What did you say? I was miles away.'

Jamie looked into her eyes. 'I said, Ned has hardly taken his eyes off you since the moment we started dancing.'

Laurel looked around the room. Ned was leaning against an upright post, two plastic glasses in his hands and he was definitely staring but whether it was at her or at Ivy, who was dancing with Harry Goode just a few feet away, she couldn't tell for sure. It was obviously Ivy he was staring at. He must have gone to get them drinks and Ivy, being Ivy, had gone to dance with someone else in the meantime.

'He's not staring at me. He's staring at Ivy.'

'Well either way, the guy does not look happy.'

'I don't understand it. He's usually pretty happy-go-lucky. I know he was terribly worried about his mum when she was ill and he didn't seem his normal self, but she's better now. And he told me, this morning, how happy he was that Ivy was coming home. Perhaps he's just tired.'

'Or perhaps he's eaten up with jealousy or guilt – or both.'

'Guilt? What's Ned done to be guilty about?'

'It might not be what he's done. It might be what he'd like to do.'

'Will you stop it!' Laurel playfully slapped his arm.

Jamie lifted her off the floor and spun her round in his arms, letting her slide slowly down the length of his body and sending sensations through her that she wasn't sure she liked. Or possibly, she liked too much.

One slow track seamlessly played into another and Laurel stayed in Jamie's arms. Since lifting her off the floor, neither of them had spoken, but once or twice, she glanced in Ned's direction. He remained against the post, the plastic cups still in his hands. Ivy was now dancing with Gabriel and Holly was making her way towards Ned. Laurel saw him put the cups down on a table and when she faced that way again, he was on the dance floor with Holly.

Jamie spun her round again, bumping into Ned and Holly in the process. 'Sorry,' Jamie said, quickly spinning her away.

Laurel looked into his eyes. 'You did that on purpose.'

He grinned. 'Did I?'

'I told you I don't like playing games.'

'I'm not playing games. I'm just not a very good dancer.'

'You seem pretty good to me.'

'I think that's the first compliment you've paid me, Laurel. Or was that sarcasm?'

'Neither. It was a fact. I think I want some air.'

She moved away from him towards the door, half expecting him to follow but when she glanced back, he was heading for the drinks tables. Why had he bumped into Holly and Ned like that? What was the purpose of it? For a moment she had actually thought… Thought what? That Jamie was enjoying the dance as much as she was? That he liked holding her in his arms as much as she liked being held? She was being foolish and it had to stop. Perhaps she should go home.

'Laurel.'

She stiffened. She would know Ned's voice anywhere. Slowly she turned to face him.

'Where's Holly? You were just dancing with her.'

'She's dancing with Gabriel.'

'But Gabriel was dancing with Ivy.'

'Well, Ivy's talking to Jamie.'

'Oh.' She couldn't think of anything else to say.

'Where were you going?' Ned looked as if that mattered.

'Oh, just outside. I wanted some fresh air. It's hot in here.' She had got to stop saying 'Oh'. It made her sound moronic.

'I'll come with you.'

'No! Oh. I mean… I'll be fine on my own.'

He frowned. 'I know you will. I'd like some fresh air

too.'

'Oh.' She *was* moronic. She glanced in Jamie's direction but he was deep in conversation with Ivy. He was so annoying. Always there when she didn't want him to be, but now that she needed him he was flirting with Ivy. She looked Ned in the eye. 'Fine. Let's go outside.'

Ned followed her to the door and held it open. To the right, there was a wooden bench and she walked towards it, unsure of what to do. She sat, and Ned sat down beside her, both staring out into the night.

'So he asked you out on a date?'

Ned's words surprised her.

'Jamie? Um. Yes.'

'When was that?'

'Er. During the May Queen Parade. We watched it from my café.'

'Did he like it?'

Laurel turned to face him. 'The parade? Or our date?'

Ned met her eyes. 'Both.'

Laurel looked away. 'Um. Well I think he liked the parade. He definitely liked the Gaggle Gang. As for our date, I couldn't say. I mean… it isn't over yet.' Why didn't she tell him it wasn't a date? She kept telling Jamie it wasn't.

'I didn't think you liked celebrities.'

'It's not that I don't like them, Ned.' She turned to face him again. 'Other than Gabriel, I don't know any. I'm just not interested in following their day-to-day lives like some people are.'

'Ivy's in to all that stuff.'

'I know she is. It's part of her job. She works with celebrities on a daily basis.'

'So she tells me.'

'Ned? Is something wrong? You don't seem… I

mean... This morning you were really happy. Has something happened? Have you... Have you had a row with Ivy?'

Ned shrugged. 'Not exactly.'

'Do you... d'you want to talk about it?'

He looked into her eyes. She grabbed the edge of the bench.

'Laurel... If I ask you something, as a friend, will you tell me the truth?'

Laurel swallowed and cleared her throat. 'Yes.'

'Were you surprised when Ivy and I started dating?'

'Yes.'

'Why?'

She was having trouble breathing. She gripped the bench tighter.

'I don't know.'

'You said you'd tell me the truth.'

'Ned. Why are you asking me this?'

'I'd like to know.'

'Why does it matter? You love her. She loves you. Isn't that enough? Does it matter what anyone else thinks?'

'Is it enough? Is it enough to love someone? Or to think you love them.'

'Yes. I think so. If you love them enough. Are you... are you having doubts?'

He stared into her eyes. 'So you won't tell me why you were surprised.'

'Only if you'll tell me why you want to know.'

'Because I value your opinion.'

'My opinion doesn't matter. It's your opinion that matters, Ned.'

'Do you think it's possible to love two people at once?'

Laurel looked away. 'Yes. I think it can be.' He was staring at her, she could feel it but she couldn't look at him again. She simply couldn't.

They sat in silence for several seconds before Ned jumped to his feet and turned to walk away. He stopped suddenly and looked back.

'You will be careful won't you, Laurel? Jamie's got a bad reputation with women, so I hear.'

'Of course I will.'

'And... you know where I am if you ever need to... talk or anything.'

Unable to speak, Laurel merely nodded.

Ned smiled wanly and turned away once more, again stopping in his tracks.

'And Laurel. I may not have said it earlier, but you are beautiful. I've always thought so. But tonight you look... well, tonight you could take a man's breath away.'

Then he was gone. And he'd taken more than her breath away.

Chapter Nineteen

'There you are.' Jamie strode towards Laurel and sat down beside her on the bench. 'I've been looking for you everywhere. Then Ned told me you were out here. Are you okay? You look... miles away.'

'I'm fine. Where's Ivy? I saw you talking to her earlier.'

'Yeah. There's definitely something going on with her and Ned. And I don't mean in a good way.'

'Oh? Did she say something to you?'

He shrugged and stretched his arms out across the back of the bench. He immediately gave a little shiver.

'It's getting chilly out here. Aren't you cold?'

Laurel shook her head. 'What did Ivy say?'

Jamie put his arm around her and pulled her towards him, encircling her with his other arm. She tried to wriggle free.

'Don't push me away. I'm trying to keep you warm.'

'Oh. Okay.' She relaxed against his body. 'But tell me what Ivy said.'

'Nothing much. It was more what she didn't say. She didn't mention Ned once. She just asked about the film business, what life was like in Hollywood, stuff like that. The usual questions people ask me. Apart from you. You haven't asked me anything like that.'

'I asked why you hit Rod Finer. And whether you'd really been dropped from the next film.'

'Yes. But you haven't asked me one question about what life is like as a Hollywood movie star or how many famous people I know.'

'And you haven't asked me one question about what life is like as a Hideaway Down café owner or who I know. What is there to ask? You go to work like everyone else. You get paid like everyone else. You go home like everyone else. Okay, perhaps your life is bigger, faster and there's more money floating about, but you still have problems like the rest of us. I'm more interested in who people are and what makes them tick than what they do.'

'And that, Laurel French, is what makes you, you.'

'Well I'm sorry to disappoint you.'

'Who said I was disappointed? So was Ned out here with you?'

Laurel nodded against his chest.

'And?'

'And what?'

He took her by the shoulders. 'Oh come on. I told you about Ivy. The least you can do is tell me about Ned.'

She shook her head. 'There's nothing to tell. Although... I think you may be right. There does seem to be a bit of tension between them. And you're right about another thing. It *is* cold out here. Let's go back inside.'

They stood up and Jamie slipped his arm around her as they headed towards the door. It seemed it was becoming a habit but he didn't take it away. It was a habit he was beginning to like.

He tried again. 'So you're not going to tell me then?' She was keeping something from him and he wanted to know what that was.

'I'll tell you this. Ned asked if I was surprised when he and Ivy started dating.'

'What did you say?'

'I said I was.'

'And?'

'There's always an 'And?' with you, isn't there? Sometimes Jamie, there is no 'And'. Sometimes there just is what there is.'

'And sometimes I don't understand a word you say. There's always more. There's always an 'And'. And if there isn't, then someone's not telling the whole story.' They walked back into the hall. 'Would you like a drink?'

Laurel tipped her head to one side and grinned at him. 'And?'

Jamie grinned back. 'And anything you want, Laurel. Anything at all.'

Suddenly she blushed. 'I'll have some May Day Punch, please. And I want to find Holly.'

'Last I saw, she was on the dance floor with Gabriel.'

'Thanks.'

Laurel headed in that direction and Jamie watched her disappear into the crowd of dancers before going to get their drinks. Something had happened between her and Ned. He was absolutely certain of it. And he wasn't sure he liked what was going through his mind.

Chapter Twenty

Laurel found Holly a few minutes later and gave her a friendly wave. She hadn't seen Ned or Ivy since coming back inside but perhaps they were sitting down somewhere, hidden by the crowd.

Holly walked towards her. 'Hi, Laurel. Are you having a good time? I couldn't believe it when Jamie told us he'd asked you out and you'd said yes. I didn't think he was your type at all. He's pretty good-looking though, isn't he?'

'He's okay. Where's Gabriel?'

'Gone to get us drinks. Where's Jamie?'

'Same. Can I ask you something, as a friend?'

Holly nodded. 'Of course. Anything.'

'Can we go and sit down somewhere? Preferably somewhere quiet.'

Holly looked around. 'I'm not sure that will be very easy. Oh, wait. I can see a couple of chairs in the corner. Are they okay?'

'Yes. They're fine.'

Laurel followed Holly to the corner chairs and they both sat down.

'What's up?'

Laurel fiddled with her dress. 'I'm not really sure how to ask this, so I'll just come out and say it. Are Ivy and Ned having problems?'

Holly held her gaze. 'What sort of problems?'

Laurel shrugged. 'I don't know. Just problems. Ned was really happy this morning when he came in for his coffee but since then he seems… well, I'm not sure. Just not himself. And a few minutes ago, Ned and I were outside and he asked me if I had been surprised when he and Ivy started dating.'

'He did?'

Laurel nodded. 'Yes. He did.'

'What did you say?'

'He asked me to tell him the truth so I did. I told him I was but I didn't say why.'

'And why were you?'

Laurel studied Holly's face. 'You mean, you weren't?'

Holly frowned. 'Maybe a little. But Ned's a lovely guy and I want my sister to be happy.'

'And is she happy?'

'Yes, I think so. She is a bit stressed today but I think that's because she had a late night and early morning, and a long drive. Other than that, I'm sure she's fine. What's this about, Laurel? What's going on?'

'I don't know, Holly. I just get the feeling that there's something wrong. Jamie's noticed it too.'

'I think Jamie's half the problem.'

'What's that supposed to mean?'

'Ivy dashed down here to see him and you know what Ned's like about Ivy's driving. Meg told Ned she had seen Ivy much earlier than Ned had expected, so I think Ned gave her a bit of a lecture.'

'That's hardly Jamie's fault.'

'Maybe not, but I think Ivy is a bit star-struck by Jamie and I think Ned may be jealous.'

'So it's because Ned is worried about Ivy, not because Ned is having second thoughts?'

'Why would Ned be having second thoughts? Did he tell you he was? What did he say to you?'

'I'm not really sure, to tell you the truth. It was all a bit strange.'

'Here come Jamie and Gabriel. We'll have to talk about this another time. Should I say something to Ivy?'

'You could find out how she feels, I suppose. And you could ask her if they've had a row. She wouldn't think it odd coming from you.'

'Okay. I'll do that. Hello, darling.' Holly smiled up at Gabriel as he handed her drink to her. 'Thanks. I'm gasping for this.'

Jamie held out a plastic glass of May Day Punch to Laurel. 'This stuff smells lethal. I hope I don't have to carry you home.'

'I'm used to it. Janet makes it every year. If anyone has to be carried home, it'll probably be you. But I won't do the carrying. That'll be Gabriel's job.'

Gabriel laughed. 'It wouldn't be the first time would it, Jamie?'

Jamie raised his glass. 'And I don't suppose it'll be the last. Here's to being carried home!'

Holly giggled. 'I'll drink to that.'

Ivy appeared from nowhere and edged her way in between Gabriel and Jamie. 'You'll drink to anything, Holly.'

'That's true. Where's Ned?'

Ivy tipped her head back. 'He's back there, talking to Kev the Rev. At least he was the last time I saw him. I may go home soon. I didn't get much sleep last night, and if I have my way, I won't be getting much tonight, either. But Ned does seem in a rather odd mood, so rampant sex might be out of the question, although I think he's just suggested exactly that. I'd better go and grab him and see. Night, all. Missing you already.'

Gabriel shook his head and smiled. 'Ivy never changes, does she? Apart from wanting an early night when there's dancing and music to enjoy. That's not like her at all.'

'I didn't hear her mention an early night,' Jamie said. 'But I did hear her mention rampant sex. Lucky Ned.'

'Lucky Ivy.' Laurel hadn't meant to say that out loud. 'I mean… We could all do with a bit of rampant sex every now and then, couldn't we?'

Jamie beamed at her. 'I'm happy to help with that.'

'I don't doubt that for a moment but I never have sex on a first date. It's my unwritten rule.'

Jamie grinned and crouched down beside her. 'So this is a date then? How many does it take?'

'In your case. About ninety-five, I should think.'

'Looks like I'll be staying here for longer than I planned in that case. And I think that may be a very good thing.'

Laurel knocked back her drink and got to her feet. 'And I think I would like to dance.'

Jamie knocked back his. 'And so would I.'

Chapter Twenty-One

'There's no need to walk me home,' Laurel said. 'You can see my front door from here, and Hideaway Down is completely safe. There's never any trouble in this village.'

'But you might trip on a paving stone or something and I would never forgive myself.' Jamie took Laurel's hand and shook his head. 'No argument. I'm seeing you home. Besides, I've parked in the car park behind the shops and the alleyway is in that direction so it's not taking me out of my way.'

'I'm not inviting you in for coffee.'

Jamie laughed. 'And you've already told me that there's no chance of rampant sex but I'm still walking you home.'

'Fine. Be a hero. But if you try to bite me on my neck, you'll get a stake through your heart. Do I make myself clear?'

'Abundantly, ma'am. That's what Adam, my vampire character would say. And then he'd rip your heart out. He's into hearts.'

'I thought they were supposed to be comedies. That doesn't sound very amusing.'

'They certainly are. Believe me, you haven't truly seen the funny side of life until your heart's been ripped out.'

'Hmm. When I heard Ned had starting dating Ivy, it felt as if my heart had been ripped out. And I didn't find it at all funny.'

'No, I don't suppose you did. That'll change though. Once Ned realises it's you he really wants.'

'But then Ivy might feel as if her heart's been ripped out.'

'What can I tell you? Love hurts sometimes. On the other hand, Ivy may feel relieved. Has it occurred to you that Ivy might not be completely in love with Ned? That she might be struggling to find a way to tell him?'

'I don't think that's likely. You heard her tonight. She couldn't wait to get him home.'

'But that was for sex, Laurel. Love and sex are two different things.'

'Maybe on your planet. But on mine, and Ivy's, and Holly's, love and sex go hand in hand.'

They reached Laurel's door and he waited whilst she opened it and turned back to face him.

'Are you telling me that you've never had a one-night stand? Or that you've never had sex with someone you weren't in love with?'

'Yes. That is, no. I've never had sex with someone I wasn't in love with, at least just a little.'

'Do you fall in love a lot?'

'No.'

'So… I take it that means you haven't had much sex?'

'I've had enough.'

'There's no such thing as 'enough' when it comes to sex.'

'Again, maybe on your planet.'

'Oh God. Don't tell me I'm dating a prude? That'll be a first for me.'

'I am *not* a prude. Just because I don't jump in and out of bed with people at the drop of a hat, doesn't make me a prude.'

He laughed. 'I think you mean, drop of someone's trousers. Or pants as we call them in the States. You should try it.'

'What?'

'Having sex with someone you're not in love with. It's very liberating.'

'How?'

'Would you like me to show you?'

Jamie moved closer and Laurel backed into the open door.

'No thanks. Just tell me.'

'There's no emotion involved. No one feels the need to say, 'I love you', or stay in bed and cuddle for a set amount of time. There're no expectations other than having a good time. You can ask the other person to do something you like without worrying about what they might think of you. It's all about fun. There's no, 'will they still love me tomorrow?' That's liberating.'

'I'm not sure how.'

'Because you've never tried it.'

'And I never shall, thanks very much. And on that note, thanks for a lovely evening. And for walking me home. Good night.'

'No kissing on the first date, either?'

'Not with you. And there won't be a second. Not that this really was a date.'

He clamped both hands to his chest. 'Ah, Laurel. You're ripping my heart out.'

'I think you have me confused with Ivy. You told me you were crazy about her.'

'So I did. Good night, Laurel. Thank you for a fabulous non-date. See you in the morning.'

Jamie turned and walked away, looking back and waving his hand in the air as he turned into the alleyway leading to the car park.

Only then did Laurel realise she had watched him walk away. She closed the door abruptly and ran up the stairs to her flat. She tossed her bag onto the sofa, kicked off her sandals and went into the kitchen to pour herself a glass of wine from the bottle she had opened earlier that evening.

She walked over to the square bay window and sat on the window seat, plumping up the cushions to place behind her back. From here, she could just see the stable door of Ned's smithy and the streetlight directly outside. A little further down was The Snowdrop Inn, its lights still blazing and one or two customers ambling from the door.

She glanced back at Ned's. If she opened the window, she could see his flat above his smithy. She'd done so once or twice before. Well, maybe more than once or twice. She wouldn't look tonight. She would rather not know if the lights were on or off.

Sipping her wine, she mulled over her conversation with Ned. Had he really said those things, or had she imagined them? Had she misconstrued his meaning? He had asked if she had been surprised about him dating Ivy. Asked about her date with Jamie. Told her he valued her opinion. Said that she knew where he was if she wanted to talk. Told her to be careful with Jamie. Said that she was beautiful, not just tonight but always. And then he had asked if she thought it was possible to be in love with two people.

One of those things was enough to give her hope but when taken all together, surely it could only mean one thing? That Jamie was right about Ned. Somehow, for some reason, Ned had suddenly realised he loved her as well as Ivy. Had he wanted her to say she loved him too? What would he have done if she had? He clearly still loved Ivy. Was that why he was miserable? Was he finding it difficult to choose?

She took several gulps of wine. This wasn't possible. It couldn't be happening. After all this time. After all these years of wanting him. Of unrequited love. Was it possible that she might someday soon find herself in Ned Stelling's powerful arms? That she might finally know what it felt like to kiss him. To be kissed *by* him. Excitement ran through her, every fibre tingling, every nerve going wild. Her knees knocked; her hands shook. And she spilt her wine right down the front of her dress.

She leapt to her feet and, pulling the dress over her head, ran into the kitchen. The sooner she put it in soak the better. Would there be any lasting damage? She loved that dress. So many wonderful things had happened this evening, because of that dress. Why hadn't she taken it off the moment she'd come in?

No point in crying over spilt milk, as Jamie had said. Or in this case, spilt wine. She would have to hope the stain would come out. The minute the shops opened on Sunday, she would nip into Eastbourne and take it to the dry cleaners. Her mum would mind the café for an hour or so. Perhaps the cleaners could work some miracle and save her 'magic' dress.

It was late and she should go to bed, but first she'd have to take her make-up off. She went into the bathroom, grabbed a cotton pad and her make-up remover and wiped at her mascara. When she finished, the pad was the colour of Jamie's bruise. Why had she suddenly thought of that? That was the second time she had thought of Jamie in less than five minutes.

Forget about Jamie, she told herself. Ned's the only one you want to think of now. But as she turned off the light, it was Jamie's face she saw in her mind's eye. And the way he had looked when they'd talked about sex. His deep, dark eyes had positively sparkled.

Chapter Twenty-Two

Laurel always opened The Coffee Hideaway at ten o'clock on Sundays but this morning she went down at eight to prepare things for her mother, taking it for granted that when she phoned her mum to ask if she would mind the café for an hour, the answer would be yes. Laurel knew it wouldn't be a problem. Her mum had done it before and on the few occasions Laurel had been ill, Trixie had manned the café until Laurel was well enough to resume work.

Laurel washed the floor with her steam mop, as she did every morning. She wiped down the tables and chairs, used her handheld vacuum on the seat cushions, and scrubbed the sink and counter until they gleamed. Every night, before she closed, she cleaned the coffee machines and cake display and turned on the dishwasher. All she had to do this morning was make the coffee and stack the crockery on the shelves, but she would do that later.

When everything was done she called her mother who said she would come straight round. Trixie wanted to hear all about last night before Laurel left for Eastbourne. Laurel made herself a coffee, sat at a table in the window and waited.

Today would be busy, but Monday would be busier. Laurel usually closed on Mondays. It was her one day off. But Monday was the May Day Parade and that was even bigger than the May Queen Parade. It was one of the highlights on the Hideaway Down village calendar. A maypole was erected in Market Field; that would go up today and after the parade and dancing around the maypole, there would be a firework display as soon as it got dark. Laurel loved fireworks. She often joked that she would have them at her wedding.

Her wedding. She had started to think that day would never happen. But now. Was there a possibility it might? Would Laurel French become Laurel Stelling? She could get used to that. Would they live above Ned's smithy or above her café? Ned's flat was definitely the larger of the two. She'd been there once or twice. Only as a friend. What would it feel like to be there as Ned's girlfriend? Better still, to be there as Ned's wife? She was letting her imagination run away with her. "Never count your chickens before they hatch," her mother often said. Perhaps she should postpone her wedding plans until after Ned actually asked her out.

But would he ask her out? He had said he was in love with two people. That didn't necessarily mean he would choose her. He might choose Ivy. Then Laurel would be back to square one. She hadn't thought of that last night. And annoyingly, when she had finally fallen asleep after tossing and turning for what seemed like hours, it hadn't been Ned she dreamt about. She'd dreamt of a vampire called Adam. A vampire who, instead of ripping out her heart, had given her his, and told her they would live as one.

Laurel shuddered at the memory. Bloody vampires. Bloody Jamie McDay. That man had really got into her head. It was probably because he irritated her so much.

And here he was again. That was definitely him walking down Market Street. She recognised the jacket. She recognised his walk. She recognised his hair.

Seconds later, he shoved open the café door.

'Morning, Laurel. I hope you slept well. Did you dream

about me?'

'Er. Can't you read the sign? It says 'Sorry. We're closed.' I don't open until ten on Sundays and it's only half past eight or so. I'm waiting for my mum. And isn't it a bit early for a Hollywood superstar to be out and about?'

He grinned and sat down opposite her, sideways on, leaning his elbow on the table and his back against the glass, his long legs stretched out in front of him.

'I'm an early riser. Always have been. You didn't answer my question.'

'I can't remember it.'

'Did you dream about me?'

'Oh that. No. I can honestly say I didn't.' Well, she wasn't lying. She didn't dream about him. She dreamt about Adam, his alter-ego.

'Pity. I dreamt about you.'

'Oh?'

'So why are you waiting for your mum?'

'She's holding the fort whilst I nip into Eastbourne.'

'Going on a shopping spree?'

'No. Tell me about your dream.'

'No. Why're you going to Eastbourne?'

'I don't think that's any of your business.'

Jamie shrugged. 'Any chance of coffee?'

'Didn't you have breakfast at Holly's?'

'No. I thought I'd have breakfast here.'

'We don't open until ten.'

Jamie laughed. 'Is there anything I can do to get you to open early? I could take you into Eastbourne.'

'I've got my own car.'

'But it would save you driving. I could buy you lunch.'

'I've got a café to run. I don't have time for lunch.' Laurel studied him for a moment. 'Did you come by car? I thought you might have walked.'

Jamie shook his head. 'One battle with that stile was quite enough for me. I won't be walking until I get some boots. I could do that today. In Eastbourne. You could help me choose some.'

'I told you, I've got a business to run.'

'If Trixie is holding the fort, why can't you ask her to stay a little longer? Have lunch with me in Eastbourne.'

'Are you asking me on a date?'

Jamie grinned. 'Would you go if I were?'

'No.'

'Then let's call it another non-date? Come on, Laurel. It might be fun.'

Laurel smiled. How could she resist that 'sad-puppy' look – even if it was completely fake? 'Okay, I'll ask my mum.'

'Great. Any chance I could have some coffee now?'

'I suppose so.' Laurel stood up. 'What would you like?'

His grin widened. 'I think I'd like a *Laurel,* please. And I've just realised. At the dance last night you said it would take about ninety-five dates before you might have sex with me. There're only ninety-three to go.'

'No. You still need ninety-five. I only count real dates. And hell will freeze over before you and I go out on one of those.'

Jamie's laughter rang out as she headed towards the counter.

'That's one of the things I like most about you, Laurel. You really know how to make a guy feel good about himself.'

'I don't think you need any help from me to feel good about yourself.'

'You're right. Most of the time I'm blissfully happy in my own skin.'

Laurel poured his coffee. 'Most of the time?'

'Even I have my off days. Like the day I punched Rod Finer. I didn't feel particularly good about myself that day.'

'So you regret it then?'

Jamie gave her an odd look. 'I regret punching him. I regret dumping Perdita the way I did. I regret getting so drunk that I did those stupid things. But on the other hand, if I hadn't done them, I wouldn't have made the snap decision to get on a plane and come here. And that I don't regret. Not at all.'

Laurel carried his coffee to the table. 'Don't stare at me. I feel like a model on a catwalk, about to take a tumble.'

'I'll catch you if you fall. Do I make you nervous?'

'What? No. Of course not. I simply meant, I don't like being on display.'

'You liked it last night.'

She placed the cup on the table. 'Yes, that's true. I did. I wouldn't lean against that glass too long, if I were you. I'm not sure how safe it is.'

'It's safety glass. It'll take my weight and a lot more besides. But it's good to know you care about me.'

'I care about my window. That's a big piece of glass to replace. Oh, great. Here comes Mum.'

Jamie sat upright. 'I thought things had improved after her reaction last night.'

Over dinner last night Laurel had, for some reason, told him what her mum had said and how she had behaved. She'd told him a lot more too. Far more than she'd told anyone before on a first date. Not that it was a date, of course.

'They have. But she wants to hear all about last night. She thinks... she thinks we were on a date. A real date.'

'And she wants the gory details.'

'Something like that, yes. And you can wipe that grin off your face right now.'

Trixie pushed the café door open and stepped inside.

'Oh! *You're* here. Good morning, Jamie.' She threw Laurel a questioning look.

'He's just arrived, Mum. He was hoping to have breakfast. He didn't realise I don't open until ten on Sundays.'

'And that wasn't my only disappointment, Mrs French.'

'Oh?' Trixie frowned at him.

Jamie got to his feet, linked Trixie's arm through his and led her towards her favourite table.

'I had such a good time last night that I asked your wonderful daughter on another date. But she tells me she can't spend the day with me because she needs to be here.'

Laurel gasped. The day? He'd said lunch. What was he playing at?

Jamie added: 'I know how much this café means to her but—'

'I can look after the café for the day, Laurel.' Trixie beamed at her. 'You know you only have to ask. It'll be fun. I've done it before and you know everything is safe with me. You two go and enjoy yourselves.'

'Er… thanks, Mum. I'll be back right after lunch.'

'No, no. You spend the day, my darling girl. You have a good time. Don't worry about me. I'll be here whenever you get back. And I can close up if you want to make an evening of it too.'

'No, I—'

'That's perfect. Thank you so much, Mrs French.'

'Oh do stop calling me that. Call me Trixie.'

'Thank you, Trixie. That's a very pretty name.'

Laurel rolled her eyes. He was really something. The nerve of the man. There was no point in arguing. She would have to spend the day with Jamie McDay. Whether she wanted to or not. Although she could always ditch him and go and see her friends.

Chapter Twenty-Three

Ivy was surprised to see Trixie behind the counter of The Coffee Hideaway. Laurel hadn't mentioned taking time off. Perhaps she was hung over after the dance last night.

'Morning, Trixie. Where's Laurel this morning?'

'Good morning, Ivy. Hello, Ned. She's out on another date with Jamie. You know, the Hollywood film star. He's taken her out for the entire day. They've gone to Eastbourne, I believe.'

Ned's grip tightened on Ivy's hand. 'They must've had a good time last night then.'

Ivy sighed. 'Wow! Lucky Laurel. An entire day with Jamie McDay.'

Ivy should be pleased for Laurel, not feel envious. She couldn't help it though. How fabulous it must be to spend the day – the entire day – in Jamie's company. Ivy had enjoyed the brief time she and Jamie spent together yesterday. Walking down from Holly Cottage, despite Jamie taking a tumble, having coffee, and then last night, chatting with him at the drinks table. She wished she'd danced with him. It would've been wonderful to be in the arms of Jamie McDay. He'd told her he wanted to but he didn't think that Ned would approve.

She'd frowned. 'I don't need Ned's approval to dance with you.'

Jamie had sighed. 'If only that were true, Ivy. But everyone keeps telling me – and you – that Ned wouldn't like this or Ned wouldn't like that. I'm beginning to think I need his permission to even talk to you. God knows how it must make you feel. And you haven't been together long from what I hear. You only started dating at Christmas.'

'It's not that bad, Jamie. You don't need his permission. *I* don't need his permission.'

'Don't you? If only I'd come to Hideaway Down for the Christmas holidays. If only you weren't dating Ned. Oh and look, he's heading in our direction again, so I think I'd better make myself scarce. I'd hate to cause an argument.'

Jamie walked away before she had a chance to respond and Ned then made things worse. Although he'd smiled and his voice had been teasing, his words had ruined the effect.

'I think it's about time you danced with me, isn't it, Ivy Gilroy?'

'I think it's about time you stopped telling me what to do!'

She'd walked away to find Jamie. She was going to ask him to dance. But she couldn't find him anywhere and Ned had followed her.

'What's going on, Ivy? Have I done something to upset you? I wasn't telling you what to do. I just want to dance with you, that's all. To hold you in my arms. Is there something wrong with that?' He'd looked like a wounded puppy.

'No, Ned. Of course not. It's just that sometimes I feel… I don't know. Like everyone is trying to control my life or something. Like everyone is watching me and… reporting back to you. Take Meg Stanbridge this morning. You got annoyed because she told you I was here and I hadn't come to see you first.'

'Yeah, I'm sorry about that. I behaved like an idiot.'

'Then you lecture me about my driving.'

'I wasn't lecturing. It's because I care.'

'I know you do. But you've got to let *me* be *me*. And then you questioned me about having coffee with Jamie. And then that business over lunch. I can't behave like someone I'm not, Ned.'

He shook his head. 'I know that, Ivy. Better than you think. I shouldn't nag you. Especially not when all I really want to do is take you in my arms and show you how I feel.'

He'd pulled her to him but Kev the Rev had interrupted to ask Ned about something he was making for the church.

Things were fine later. When she'd suggested an early night, Ned had instantly agreed. That was exactly what they needed, he'd told her. To spend more time together. And it had been wonderful. But then sex with Ned was always wonderful. Sex had been perfect from the start. It was all the other stuff they needed to work on.

'Ivy, dear.' Trixie was waving her hand in front of Ivy's face. 'I asked if you wanted a doughnut with your coffee. I know how much you like them.'

'Sorry. I was trying to decide what I wanted and I think I finally have. I think it's time I tried something different. I'll have one of those chocolate sparkles, please. The one right there with all the glitter on. The more glittery the better as far as I'm concerned.'

'I'm with you on that, dear. One can't beat a bit of glitter, especially if it's edible. What would you like, Ned?'

'I'll have one of Laurel's homemade buns please, Trixie. The ones with all the ginger bits on top.'

'Coming right up. Take a seat you two and I'll bring them over with your coffee.'

Ivy sauntered to a table near the window, removed her suede jacket and took a seat.

'So Laurel's dating a Hollywood superstar. Who'd have guessed it?'

Ned pulled out a chair and sat beside her.

'Certainly not me. Laurel's not into all that celebrity nonsense.'

Ivy tutted. 'It's not nonsense, Ned.'

'No. I'm sorry.' Ned fiddled with a coaster, turning it around in his fingers. 'What I meant was, Laurel wouldn't be influenced by that. She wouldn't be swept off her feet just because the guy's a film star.'

Ivy flopped back in her chair. 'I would. And Holly's dating a famous author. It's funny, isn't it? Laurel's not in the least bit interested in celebrity status and neither is my sister, whereas I'm surrounded by celebrities on a daily basis and I love it. And yet they're the ones dating famous people.'

Ned banged the coaster flat. 'Whereas you're just dating a blacksmith.'

Ivy blinked. 'Well yes. But I didn't mean it in the way you're making it sound. What I meant was… how strange it is that we're all dating people we wouldn't have expected to. No, that didn't sound right either. I mean we're all dating people who're our opposites in many ways.'

'I know exactly what you mean.'

'Oh God. You're not cross again, are you?'

Ned shook his head. 'No, Ivy. I'm not cross. You're right. In many ways it would make more sense for you to be the one going out with Jamie and for Laurel to be going out with… well, me, I suppose.'

'You're right, Ned. Laurel and you are far more suited in so many ways than you and me.'

'And I suppose, so are you and he. Jamie, I mean.'

Ivy gave him a playful nudge. 'Perhaps we should

switch.'

Ned didn't look up but she could see the muscles tighten in his jaw. 'Perhaps we should. Is that what you want?'

He was serious. Dear God. The man had actually thought about it. But then, so had she. Over the last few weeks she thought rather a lot about whether she and Ned were really suited to one another. And even more so since she arrived yesterday.

'I don't know, Ned. Is that what *you* want?'

Now he did look at her. 'I just want you to be happy, Ivy. And I'd like to be happy too. If that means... well, if that means us breaking up then... then I suppose it's better to do it sooner rather than later, isn't it? For everyone concerned.'

Was this happening? Was this really happening? Was Ned Stelling dumping her?

'Yes. I suppose it is. Are you saying it's over then? Between us, I mean.'

'If that's what you want.'

'I... I love you, Ned. You do know that, don't you?'

He nodded. 'I love you too. But sometimes that's just not enough, is it?'

'No. Apparently not. Okay. If that's the way it is, then I don't suppose there's much point in me sitting here, is there?'

'I'll go. You stay. I've got lots of work to catch up with. I may as well make a start.' He got to his feet. 'Ivy. You know I'll always be here for you, don't you. If you... if you need me.'

'Same here.' She couldn't look at him. 'I'll always be your friend. Always, Ned.'

'Take care.'

'And you. Bye.'

She wanted to run after him but what was the point. They were as different as chalk and cheese. They wanted completely different things. It had been fun while it lasted. But now it was over and they were both free to move on. Both free to find someone more suitable. She swiped away a tear and then another. She hadn't expected it to feel so bad.

'Oh. Where's Ned gone?' Trixie stood beside her, holding a tray with their coffees and cakes.

'Back to his smithy.'

'Will he be coming back?'

'No, Trixie. He's moving on to someone better.'

'To someone…? Oh good heavens. Has something happened between the two of you? Have you split up?'

'Yes, Trixie. We have. And I don't want to be rude, but I need to get out of here.'

Ivy leapt to her feet and dashed towards the door. Where could she go? Her car was at Ned's, and her mum's pub was virtually opposite Ned's smithy. She glanced towards Holly's empty shop. Holly must still be at home. Ivy turned and ran as fast as she could in the direction of Holly Cottage.

Chapter Twenty-Four

By the time Ivy arrived at Holly Cottage she had stopped crying. Partly because she had run out of tears and partly because she could hardly breathe. The row of four cottages, of which Holly Cottage was one, had seemed to get further away as she climbed the steep gradients of the grassy meadows and clambered over not just one but three, still slippery, stiles. Having shoved the front door open, Ivy stumbled into the kitchen and collapsed in the armchair beside the Rayburn.

Gabriel, who was making coffee, gave her an odd look. 'Good morning, Ivy. Would you like some coffee?'

Unable to speak and panting for breath, Ivy nodded in response.

Holly dashed into the kitchen and pinched Ivy on the arm, followed by a gentle punch.

Ivy managed a strangled yelp.

'A pinch and a punch for the first of the month. It's the first of May today. Oh! What's wrong with you? You look awful? Your face is all red and your eyes are all puffy.'

Ivy rubbed her arm and sucked in a large breath.

'Ned's just dumped me.'

'What?' Holly and Gabriel spoke in unison.

Holly knelt down in front of Ivy and took her hands in hers. 'Why? What happened?'

Ivy shook her head.

'I'll make coffee. Unless you'd rather I left.' Gabriel hovered by the worktop.

Ivy shook her head again. 'Stay.'

Holly straightened up. 'Forget coffee. Where's The Monk's Medicine, Gabriel? And a large glass please.'

Gabriel rummaged in a cupboard and a few seconds later, Holly was handing Ivy a tumbler, half full of brandy.

'Drink this. Gramps always says that there's nothing better than The Monk's Medicine to cure all the problems of the world.'

Ivy took the glass and knocked the contents back. She choked several times as she held out the glass for Holly to take.

Holly slapped her on the back and Ivy finally caught her breath.

'Thanks,' Ivy croaked.

Holly smiled. 'You're welcome.'

She pulled up a chair, and one for Gabriel and patted the seat cushion. Gabriel came and sat beside her, carrying two more glasses and the brandy bottle. When each glass was full Holly squeezed one of Ivy's hands.

'Tell us what happened.'

Before Ivy could speak, they heard a screech of tyres, someone running across the gravel and the door of Holly Cottage bursting open. Ivy lifted her head. Was it Ned? Had he come to find her?

'Ivy!'

It was her mum's voice and Ivy sank back into the chair.

'She's in here, Mum,' Holly yelled.

Janet raced into the kitchen. 'I came as soon as I heard. My poor darling.'

Gabriel stood up, and moved his chair next to Ivy's for Janet to sit down whilst he found another for himself.

'Who told you?' Ivy asked, her eyes again filling with tears.

Janet wrapped her arms around her. 'Trixie. She

phoned me the moment you left but I was down in the cellar and Gramps took the call. He tripped over Mistletoe in his haste to get me and for a moment I thought he'd twisted his ankle but he's fine. I had to get him settled before I came here. That's why it's taken me so long. So tell me. What's happened? All I know is that you and Ned have broken up. Has this got something to do with that Jamie McDay? I knew he was trouble. Wait till I get my hands on him.'

Gabriel frowned. 'What's Jamie got to do with it? I thought he was dating Laurel.'

Janet glared at him. 'I think he's keeping his options open. It was pretty clear to me that it's Ivy he's got his eye on. Told me a lot of nonsense yesterday lunchtime, hoping to put doubt in my mind. I suppose he thought I'd pass it on to Ivy and do his dirty work for him. Did he say something to Ned, darling? Is that what happened?'

'No!' Ivy screeched. 'Jamie hasn't said anything. He…'

But he had said something. Ivy wiped her eyes. Yesterday, in this very cottage and then on the walk to the village. He'd said more in The Coffee Hideaway and again at the dance. He'd added to her own doubts about her relationship with Ned.

'I've known Jamie for most of my life, Janet, and whilst I'll be the first to agree that he can be a bit of a bastard where women are concerned, I'm sure he wouldn't set out to break up a relationship.' Gabriel didn't sound pleased. 'Unless of course he could see that the relationship wasn't going anywhere. Then I suppose he might say something.'

'Are you saying Ivy and Ned's relationship wasn't going anywhere?' Holly asked.

'Well, it clearly wasn't, was it? They've just broken

up.'

Janet gave a loud tut. 'Because of your friend!'

Ivy couldn't listen to this. 'Stop it. Just stop it! We didn't break up because of Jamie. Ned dumped me because he doesn't think we're very well suited. And I have to agree with him. We're not. If he hadn't ended things with me then... then I'd have ended it. Eventually. We want different things. I love London. Ned hates it. I love my career. Ned doesn't understand why I'm so taken with celebrities, and parties, or why I love champagne when he can't stand the stuff. That's why we've split up. Not because of Jamie. Okay?'

Janet's mouth fell open. 'Well, okay then, darling. If that's the way it was then no one's really to blame, I suppose. But Ned knew what you were like before he—'

'Stop it, Mum. Don't start trying to blame Ned for this. I knew just as well as he did how completely opposite we are. In every single way. It's nobody's fault. It's... it's just upsetting, that's all. Very, very upsetting, in fact. I feel like shit! Gabriel! Where's that brandy?'

'It's here, Ivy. It's right here.' He filled her glass. 'Janet? One for you?'

She nodded and finally smiled. 'Yes please, Gabriel. And I apologise for what I said about your friend.'

Gabriel returned her smile. 'And I'm sorry I took that tone with you. I'd have felt the same if I were in your place.'

Holly kissed him on the cheek. 'I'm sorry, too, darling, for snapping at you.'

'And *I'm* sorry that I'm not more like Laurel.' Ivy emptied her glass and held it out for yet another refill.

'What? Why?' Holly frowned at the empty glass.

'Because then maybe Ned would really love me. We'd certainly have so much more in common. In fact, I even joked that we should swap partners. Ned should be with Laurel and I should be with Jamie.'

Gabriel coughed. 'Er… Was that before or after he dumped you, Ivy?'

'Before, I think. Why? It's not as if it matters now, is it? I'm suddenly really tired. Holly, can I crash on Jamie's bed?'

She stood up and wobbled until Gabriel held her still.

'You can crash on ours. I'll take you up.'

Holly nodded her agreement and Gabriel lifted Ivy in his arms and carried her upstairs.

'Ned did this last night,' Ivy said. 'But I wasn't drunk. Oh Gabriel, I can't believe I'll never be in Ned's arms again.'

'Don't worry, Ivy. Things may look bad now, but they might look very different when you wake up.'

'Things look very different now, Gabriel. Since when has Holly Cottage had two flights of stairs?'

'Since you drank several large glasses of brandy, I would say.'

Chapter Twenty-Five

Laurel glanced at her phone as the sound of tinkling chimes announced the arrival of not just one text message but two, one almost immediately after the other. She couldn't check them straight away as her fingers were covered in sticky barbecue sauce, from the spare ribs she was eating without a knife and fork.

'Someone's eager to get hold of you,' Jamie said. 'I hope nothing's happened at the café that requires your attention.'

'I think Mum's capable of handling almost anything. I'd better check though, just in case.'

She dunked her fingers in the bowl of warm water and lemon juice on the table in front of her and wiped them dry with a couple of paper towels from the pile provided. She picked up her phone and opened the first text which was indeed from her mother.

'Oh my God!'

'What is it? What's happened?' Jamie sounded concerned.

'It's... it's Ned. He... he's just dumped Ivy. It's from Mum. She says they were in the café when it happened. One minute they were ordering coffee and cake and the next, Ivy's about to burst into tears, and Ned is walking out. Oh Jamie, I can't believe it. I never thought he'd do it. Not really. Not deep down. When he told me yesterday I...' She had said too much. Perhaps Jamie wouldn't pick up on it.

'I can't believe it either. But it seems you had an idea

that this might happen. Is that what you two were talking about outside on the bench last night? Did Ned tell you how he feels? Did you tell him how you feel about him?'

'Not exactly. I mean... it was such a strange conversation. He didn't tell me how he felt. Why are you looking at me like that? He didn't!'

'What *did* he tell you?'

'Um. He asked if I'd been surprised about him dating Ivy. I told you that last night. He said he valued my opinion. Then he asked a bit about my date with you. Said that if I ever wanted to talk I knew where he was. He also told me to be careful with you.'

'Hmm. He doesn't like me very much, does he?'

'Perhaps he knew you were after his girlfriend. Oh! I suppose... I suppose this means that Ivy's free now. You... you've got your wish.'

'So it would appear. And you've got yours. Tell me what else he said last night.'

'Er.'

'There's no need to be shy, Laurel. Your secret's safe with me. What did he say?'

Laurel met his eyes. They seemed colder somehow.

'He asked if I thought it was possible to be in love with two people at once.'

'Did he? And what did you say to that?'

'I can't remember. I think I said yes.'

'And?'

'And that was it.'

'Are you sure?'

'Yes. Oh. Apart from that he thought I was beautiful, not just last night but always. And that I could take a man's breath away. I was so shocked, I couldn't think of anything to say. He was walking away at the time.'

'Was he? That's odd.'

'Why?'

'Because if I'd just said that to the woman I loved, I'd have pulled her into my arms and shown her just how beautiful I thought she was. Breath or no breath.'

'Well, Ned's not you. Besides, he was still dating Ivy when he said that and Ned unlike you, doesn't date more than one woman at a time.'

'No. He just tells them how beautiful they are and how they take his breath away. I can't see the difference really. Except I'm more open and honest about what I'm doing. If I'm dating more than one woman at a time, I tell them.' He grinned suddenly. 'All eight of them. I mean, it's only fair they all know where they stand.'

Laurel gasped. 'You are unbelievable!'

'So I'm told. And you haven't even been to bed with me yet.'

'And I won't be. Ever.'

He became serious. 'No. I suppose you'll be dating Ned by this time tomorrow. We've both done what we came here for. I'll take you back as soon as we've finished lunch.'

'Oh, I thought... Yes. Yes, of course. I want to find out exactly what's happened. And you, no doubt, want to find Ivy and ask her out.'

'Something like that. Yes. You'd better check the second text. It might be from Ned.'

'It's from Holly. I saw her name flash up.' Laurel opened the text. 'Ivy's at Holly's. Gabriel's just taken her upstairs so that she can get some sleep. She's pretty upset. So much for your theory that Ivy was looking for a way to dump Ned. She may not want to go out with you. No. We both know she will. She's had a crush on you for years. She told me that yesterday morning when she first arrived.'

'You didn't tell me that.'

'Your ego was big enough already.' She prodded her food with her fork. 'I'm not very hungry anymore. This whole thing has taken away my appetite.'

'Having second thoughts?'

'About what?'

'About Ned.'

'No I… It just feels wrong somehow. I didn't want it to be like this.'

'We should be careful what we wish for.'

Laurel nodded. 'I think I feel guilty. If Ivy is upset, that must surely mean she didn't plan to end things with Ned, mustn't it?'

'Not necessarily. Sometimes you can love someone but believe you're not right for them. You'd be upset, but you'd want what's best for them. You want them to be happy, even if their happiness means you being miserable.'

'Wow! I don't suppose that's something you'd ever do, is it? Have you ever been in love with anyone? Really in love? Head over heels in love?'

'Like you think you are with Ned, you mean? Or like Gabriel is with Holly? No. I've never felt like that. Apart from in my movies. But I suppose that doesn't count.'

Laurel laughed. 'No, Jamie. I'm talking about real life.'

He scooped up a forkful of his beef stroganoff but left it where it was. 'I think I've lost my appetite too. It must be all this excitement. You and Ned, together after all these years. Are you ready to go? I'll take you back to Hideaway Down now.'

Laurel nodded. 'If you're sure you've finished.'

'Yes, Laurel. I think I can definitely say I'm finished. I'll get the bill.'

Chapter Twenty-Six

Laurel's heels clicked against the black and red tiles in the aisle of the nave of St Catherine's Church. She had asked Jamie to drop her outside on the pretext of having to speak to Kev the Rev about something in the May Day Parade. Jamie hadn't asked for details, which in itself came as quite a surprise. Until about an hour ago, he'd had questions about everything, or so it seemed. Since leaving the restaurant, he had hardly said a word and when he pulled up outside the church, it was as if he couldn't wait to be rid of her. He was obviously in a hurry to get to Holly Cottage and persuade Ivy to go on a date with him.

'Hello, Laurel. This is a lovely surprise. Have you come to see me?' The Reverend Kevin Longbourne always had a cheerful smile and a welcome in his voice. And a brightly coloured T-shirt with Kev the Rev emblazoned on the front. Today, the words were in white and the T-shirt, multi-coloured. 'I'm between sermons and was about to have a cup of tea. Would you like to join me? Or are you in a rush to get back to your café? I hear Trixie's doing a fine job in your stead.'

Laurel smiled. 'I'm not in a rush and I would like to talk, if that's okay with you? I know I'm not a regular churchgoer, but I could use a friendly ear. And an impartial one.'

'God is always happy to listen, Laurel, whether you come to church or not. And so am I. Let's nip next door to the rectory and I'll put the kettle on. I think I've even got some chocolate digestives. But don't tell Audrey, will you? She says I've been eating too many chocolate biscuits while she's been away.'

'Has she come back to help out, then? I know she was feeling much better, but I didn't realise she had resumed her church activities.'

'She hasn't. But she came to Sunday service and gave me a good telling off.'

'She's definitely feeling better then.'

Laurel followed the Reverend out through the side door of the church, down a narrow path with daffodils and irises lining both sides, and into the boot room of the rectory.

'Go through into the sitting room and I'll be with you shortly.'

Laurel took a seat on the sunflower-yellow sofa and waited for him to join her which he did in a matter of minutes, carrying a tray with tea cups, a tea cosy-covered teapot, a bowl of sugar and a jug of milk, together with a plate of chocolate digestives. He set it down on the coffee table and sat opposite her on a red, leather wingback chair.

'Help yourself to a biscuit, and begin when you're ready. I'll pour the tea.'

Laurel cleared her throat and twiddled her thumbs in her lap. 'I'm not really sure where to start. Or even what I want to say. I just feel so confused and I honestly didn't know who else to talk to. I hope you don't mind.'

He smiled by way of an answer and handed her a cup of tea. Taking a chocolate digestive which he balanced on his saucer, he sat back in his chair.

'I suppose you've heard that Ned has ended his relationship with Ivy today.'

Kev the Rev nodded. 'Yes. I'm afraid it's all over the village. That sort of news travels fast.'

'Well, I may as well just come out and say it. I've been

in love with Ned for my entire life. It was unrequited. At least I thought it was. And somehow that made it even more intense. Then yesterday, Ned gave me reason to believe that he may have feelings for me. Nothing happened. It was just something he said. And to be honest, I was over the moon. I'd almost booked our wedding.' She gave a little laugh. 'Sorry. That wasn't funny. The thing is, when I got the texts from Mum and Holly telling me what had happened, I felt guilty. As if I'm to blame in some way. And I'm not. Truly, I'm not.'

'I'm sure you're not. I'm sure this has nothing to do with you, Laurel. Their break-up, that is. These things happen to the best of us. There is no right or wrong. And you shouldn't feel guilty for loving someone, unless you act in a deceitful manner. And I know that's something you would never do.'

'I'm not so sure. I pretended to go on a date with someone because he told me it might make Ned jealous. And that's what seems to have happened. Ned saw us together and suddenly decided he didn't want to be with Ivy any longer. Ned asked me last night if I thought it was possible to be in love with two people at the same time, and I said yes.'

'Ah. This must be the film star I've heard so much about. Jamie McDay, isn't it?'

'Yes.'

'And you only pretended to be on a date?'

'Yes.'

'Did you enjoy this date?'

'Well... Yes. Jamie's fun to be with. But that's the other thing, you see. Jamie fancies Ivy.'

'He told you that?'

'Yes. From the very start. I can't believe it was only yesterday morning. He's just dropped me off. I think he's going to ask Ivy out.'

'And does that bother you?'

Laurel hesitated. Did it bother her? Of course it did. Her mother would be furious. She was so pleased that her daughter was dating a Hollywood movie star.

'Um. I think it does a little. Yes. But not because I like him. And not because I'm jealous. Just because… Well, I don't know really. Just because. And Mum will be disappointed.'

Laurel grabbed a biscuit. She needed something sweet.

'Do you think you have feelings for him?'

Laurel swallowed her mouthful. 'For Jamie? No. He's arrogant. He's got an answer for everything. He's dated more women than I've got freckles. And none of them were serious. He's probably lost his job, but he doesn't seem that bothered. And he'll be going back to Hollywood as soon as things die down. Oh… I wonder if he'll take Ivy with him.'

'Would it bother you if he did?'

'I… No, I… I don't want to talk about Jamie, if you don't mind. I need to talk about Ned. I don't know what to do.'

'Has Ned asked you out?'

'I haven't seen him since it happened. Jamie and I were in Eastbourne having lunch. I came straight here.'

'Well, Laurel. Firstly, you have nothing to feel guilty about. Perhaps it wasn't such a good idea to pretend to date Jamie in the hope of making Ned jealous but Ned wouldn't be jealous if he didn't have feelings for you. If what you say is correct, Ned has done the right thing by ending his relationship with Ivy before asking you out. Of course, Ivy may be upset if you go out with Ned, but neither of you would be doing anything wrong, and I'm sure Ivy will see that. Perhaps if Jamie does start dating

Ivy, everything will work out for the best. Providing, that is, you wouldn't be jealous of Ivy being with Jamie.'

'No. No I wouldn't be jealous at all. Not at all.'

'Then the only thing I can say is that you'll have to see how things turn out. Perhaps you could talk to Ned and wait for a few days before you start dating one another. Or simply wait and see if Ned asks you out. He may not feel the time is right. After all, if you've waited this long for him, a few more days can't hurt.'

'You're right. And that's exactly what I'll do. Thank you so much, Reverend. And thank you for the tea and biscuits. I'd better get back and help Mum. I feel so much better now. As if a weight has been lifted from my shoulders.'

'I'm not sure I was very much help, but I'm pleased you're feeling better. My door is always open, Laurel. Enjoy your afternoon.'

'Thank you, Reverend. You too.'

Laurel turned left from the rectory instead of right. She wasn't quite ready to face her mum. What she needed was a walk. A walk across the meadows and the pastures of Hideaway Farm. In the distance, Henry Goode was tending sheep. She would recognise him anywhere. It looked like Harry was helping out as he often did on Sundays, and on weekdays once he'd finished delivering the milk. She would recognise Harry from a mile away, too.

What a glorious spring day it was. And the first of May. She'd completely forgotten that. A new month; a fresh start. That's what her mother often said. Well, that was certainly true for Ned and Ivy. And possibly, Jamie too. And herself, of course. This was a new month and a fresh start for her. How could so much change in such a short space of time? There was a song about the difference a day could make. She couldn't remember the tune, or the words come to that. Ivy would remember. Ivy was always singing. Ivy was…

Oh God. Was Ivy miserable? Kev the Rev had told her it wasn't her fault. But was that really true? Jamie had said we should be careful what we wish for. That was definitely true. And why had she gone to see the vicar, anyway? She wasn't religious. She hardly ever went to church. Was it just because she felt so guilty? Was it even guilt? Or was it something else entirely? Something she wasn't ready to admit. Not to the vicar. Not even to herself. Why had her life suddenly become such a complete and utter mess?

Chapter Twenty-Seven

Laurel couldn't settle, no matter what she did. It was only seven p.m. but it felt as if time itself had slowed down. She switched on the TV, flicked through the channels and switched it off. She went to clean the kitchen but remembered she'd already done it. Twice. She tried to read, only to discard the book six pages in, having realised she hadn't taken in one word. What on earth was wrong with her? She poured herself more wine and paced the room, glass in hand.

She had hoped the two-hour walk she had taken after leaving the vicarage would have helped clear her head but ever since returning to The Coffee Hideaway at four o'clock, she'd felt even more restless. She had listened to her mum's opinions and advice but she hadn't mentioned her conversation with the vicar. Nor had she told her mum about the ones with Ned last night, and with Jamie today. She loved her mother dearly but some things were better not discussed with Trixie French.

After her mother left for home, Laurel stayed for an hour to tidy up. She'd mopped the floor, cleaned the sink and counter, wiped the tables and loaded the dishwasher. Every five minutes, she had glanced towards the window, half expecting to see either Ned or Jamie approach. But neither of them had. She hadn't seen Holly or Gabriel and of course, there was no sign of Ivy. In fact, she hadn't seen anyone she knew, and that in itself was strange. It was as if the village had turned into a ghost town. Everyone, it seemed, was staying indoors… or had all gone to the pub early.

When she'd done all she could in the café, she'd gone upstairs and cleaned the kitchen, forgetting she hadn't yet had supper. She made herself some, only to throw it away, and cleaned the kitchen again before running a bath. But her attempts to relax had all proved futile.

This was ridiculous. She had to do something. She had to make a decision; take her own life in her hands. For once, she would do what her mother had been telling her to do for years: go to see Ned Stelling and tell him how she really felt.

Nervous energy gnawed at her skin as she threw on a clean dress; the one she was wearing earlier having been consigned to the laundry bin. She quickly brushed her hair, slipped on her shoes and dashed downstairs. Taking a deep breath, she closed her front door and hurried down Market Street, to Ned's, which took her a total of around five minutes. There was hardly anyone about even now. People were usually walking their dogs, or going to the pub or visiting friends at seven-thirty on a Sunday evening but, apart from a couple whom she'd never seen before – visitors walking through the village – she saw no one she knew.

She glanced across to The Snowdrop Inn, the door of which was firmly closed even though it was obviously open for business: all the lights were on and the usual sounds of chatting customers and music from the radio crept towards her on the evening breeze. She took another deep breath and rang Ned's bell.

His face was full of hope as he flung open the door, but it was fleeting and rapidly replaced by a veil of despondence.

'Oh. It's you. Sorry. Hello, Laurel. Is everything okay?'

'You tell me, Ned. It certainly doesn't look it from where I'm standing. May I come in?'

'Unless it's something urgent, can it wait until tomorrow? I've had a few drinks and I won't be good company. Have you heard? It's over between Ivy and me.'

'This is Hideaway Down, Ned. The entire village has heard. That's why I'm here. Now please, may I come in?'

'I don't want to talk about it, Laurel. Not tonight. I can't.'

'I think we should, Ned. And the sooner the better.'

He let out a tortuous sigh and stood aside to let Laurel pass. 'Upstairs,' he said, pointing upwards.

Laurel made her way upstairs and into Ned's sitting room.

'Want a drink? I'm having one.'

'It looks as if you've had several already.'

'Tut-tut, Laurel.' He wagged a finger at her. 'You shouldn't lecture. People don't like being lectured to. Ivy hates it.'

'Sorry. I didn't mean it to sound like a lecture.'

'That's what I always tell Ivy.'

'Ned. Will you please sit down? I need to talk to you.'

'Has Jamie dumped you?'

That took her by surprise. 'Um. In a way I suppose he has. Yes.'

'Is he going to go out with Ivy now?'

'I think he would like to. But that really depends on Ivy.'

'Oh, Ivy wants to. Ivy wants to very much.'

'Does she? Are you sure? Ned. Please sit down. I need to ask you a question.'

He slumped into a chair and emptied his glass. 'Fire away.'

'Why did you end your relationship with Ivy? It wasn't

because of me, was it?'

From the look on his face, he wasn't expecting that. He shook his head.

'No. It was because it wouldn't work. No matter how much I wanted it to, it just wouldn't. And then Jamie arrived. And I knew it was over.'

'Ned? Do you have feelings for me?'

'Of course I do. I love you, you know that. I've been friends with you my entire life.'

'Yes. But I don't mean as friends. I mean… Do you *love* me?'

His eyes narrowed and he stared at her for several seconds. 'I… I don't know. I could. I know I could. You and I are more alike. We have things in common, you and me. Not like me and Ivy. We have nothing in common. Sorry. *Had* nothing in common.'

Laurel sighed. It was a sigh of relief. That came as a surprise.

'Ned, last night at the dance, you said some things that made me think you were having doubts about Ivy. I thought you were telling me, in a roundabout way, that you were in love with two people. You were in love with Ivy. And possibly with me?'

He screwed up his eyes and then opened them wide. He was clearly having trouble focusing.

'Did I say that? I don't remember. I know I was concerned about you seeing Jamie. And I knew Ivy was in love with him. Sorry. *Is* in love with him. I don't want you to get hurt. You deserve better than that.'

'Ned. Please listen to me. Ned. Ned!'

He shook himself awake. 'Laurel, I think I need to go to bed.'

'What the hell was that?'

Laurel jumped to her feet and ran to the window. A

horn was blasting. Someone was screaming. Geese were screeching and cackling. Suddenly, the village was alive. People were running towards Ned's door. Laurel threw open the window and looked below. Smoke was drifting upwards from the crumpled bonnet of a car wrapped around the street lamp right in front of Ned's door.

'Oh my God! Ned! Ned!'

He sat bolt upright.

'Ned. It's Ivy. She's smashed her car into the lamppost.'

Laurel couldn't believe her eyes. Ned moved faster than lightning. Before she had taken three running steps towards the stairs, Ned was down them and out into the street.

'Call an ambulance,' he yelled back at Laurel.

Laurel was already dialling. She gave directions and details and kept the line open as they requested.

Meg Stanbridge stood just a few feet away, as white as a sheet. Laurel ran to her as Ned tugged at the car door.

'What happened, Meg? Are you okay?'

Meg didn't answer. She simply shook her head. People poured out from the pub and Laurel waved to Henry Goode.

'Henry! Get Janet. It's Ivy. There's been an accident.'

'Nearly killed the geese, she did.' Meg's voice was little more than a whisper.

'What happened?'

'Came from nowhere, she did. Lordy, Lordy me. I thought my babies were goners but she swerved at the last minute, she did. Swerved so as not to hit them. Caught one by the tail though.' Meg held up a solitary white feather. 'No permanent damage.'

Janet Gilroy screamed and raced down the bank.

'Stay back,' Ned told her. 'I've almost got the door

open.'

Henry arrived with Harry just as the door gave out, the sound of metal on metal buckling under Ned's determined force.

Ned gingerly lifted Ivy's head from the inflated airbag, after gently feeling his way, finger by finger down her neck, her spine and across her shoulders to try to see if anything was broken.

'Ivy? Ivy, darling. Can you hear me?'

Ivy's lashes flickered. 'Ned? Her voice was low and rasping. 'Ned, is that you?'

'Yes, Ivy. It's me. Don't try to talk any more. Don't try to move. The ambulance will be here soon.'

Ivy's lashes flickered again and Ned's eyes searched frantically about as if seeking some divine intervention.

Laurel stood close by, one arm around Meg's shoulder, the other arm linked through Gramps' as Janet knelt by Ned, stroking her daughter's bloodstained hair. Everyone in the village had now come out to see what was going on.

'Someone should phone Holly,' Gramps whispered.

'Of course. I'll call her.' Laurel dialled Holly's number and told her friend the terrible news.

Chapter Twenty-Eight

Where *was* that ambulance? Ned prayed for it to hurry up, at the same time praying for Ivy to be okay. Then he did what everyone did at times like these: bargained with some unseen power. If Ivy could come out of this with bruises and cuts but otherwise unscathed, he would do anything. Give anything. Finally, the sirens wailed and rapidly grew louder. The ambulance was here.

Reluctantly, Ned moved away, along with Janet, but only as far as necessary to allow the ambulance crew to do their work. Ned held Janet tightly, neither speaking as Ivy was slowly eased from the driver's seat onto a stretcher. Holly arrived just as Ivy was placed into the ambulance and Janet was climbing in beside her.

'What's happened? Is she okay? Will Ivy be okay?'

Janet reached out to Holly, her eyes full of tears. 'We think so. They say they won't know for sure until they get her to the hospital. I'll see you there.' The ambulance doors closed and the sirens wailed into the night.

'Can I go with you to the hospital, Holly?' Ned was desperate. He couldn't drive. He'd had too much to drink. But he had to get to the hospital.

'Yes. Yes, Ned. Of course you can.'

Laurel stepped forward. 'May I come too? And Gramps is here.'

It was Gabriel who answered this time. 'Yes. The car's just there.'

He pointed to the car a few feet away and all five of them piled in, Ned providing Gramps with some assistance. The ambulance had raced ahead but Gabriel drove as fast as he safely could and they arrived as Ivy was being wheeled into a cubicle and the curtain drawn around her.

Ned paced up and down the waiting room, desperate for news. Once or twice someone handed him a plastic cup of coffee but he wasn't quite sure whom. He gratefully drank it and paced some more.

Minutes felt like hours; hours felt like days but in reality it was probably only a couple of hours until a doctor informed them that, other than a broken ankle and several cuts and bruises, Ivy would be fine. She was lucky, so he said.

Ned could finally breathe again.

'May I see her?' Janet asked. 'She's my daughter.'

The doctor nodded. 'Yes. She's awake but drowsy. We've given her something for the pain. We're keeping her in for a day or two, just in case of concussion, but we're sure there's nothing to worry about.'

'Other than the police,' Gabriel whispered.

'Police?' Ned didn't understand. 'It was an accident. No one was hurt apart from Ivy and she'd only driven from the rear yard into Market Street – just a few metres. Why does she need to worry about the police? Oh. She was speeding?'

Gabriel nodded. 'Probably. But that's not what I meant. She'd also been drinking. She had several glasses of brandy when she came to us this morning.'

'Brandy? The only time Ivy drinks brandy is when she's really upset.'

'Precisely. She was very, very upset. Oh shit! I'm not trying to put this on you, Ned. Believe me, I'm not. We didn't even know she'd left. We thought she was still asleep upstairs on our bed. We had no idea she'd come down here to get her car. How did she manage to hit the lamp post? Had you had another row?'

'No! I haven't seen Ivy since morning. I was with Laurel. I mean, Laurel was with me. We were talking when we heard the crash. What do you mean Ivy was very upset? I thought she'd be happy.'

'Happy? Why the fuck would she be happy? She'd just been dumped by the man she loves.'

'What? Are you saying that bastard Jamie dumped her?'

'What? Of course I'm not. What's Jamie got to do with it? I'm talking about you, you idiot. You're the one who dumped her.'

'I didn't dump her! She told me she wanted to be with Jamie. She told me we had nothing in common. It broke my heart to get up and leave but I couldn't stay and talk about him.'

Gabriel stared at him in disbelief. 'You twit. You fucking, stupid twit. Ivy's not in love with Jamie! She's infatuated with the character he plays and yes, she thinks he's gorgeous and she's had a crush on him for years, apparently, but millions of other women feel the same. Did you honestly believe that Ivy wanted to be with him? Is that really why you dumped her?'

'I didn't dump her. We talked about it. We discussed how different we are. We... Oh shit. I thought she loved him. I thought she loved us both. But I can't compete with him. And I thought she made that clear. Did I completely misunderstand?'

Gabriel shook his head. 'I wasn't there. So I have no idea. All I can tell you is that she came to us in tears and told us that you'd dumped her. And believe me, Ned, she was heartbroken. She may have tried to pretend she wasn't when she was with you, but she was crushed.'

'But I don't understand. She kept saying how different we are. Kept getting annoyed because I nagged her about her driving. Said I kept trying to tell her what to do.'

'That's true. She did. She said something similar to us. But what you've got to understand, Ned, is that Ivy hadn't planned to fall head over heels in love with you at Christmas. She loves her job. She loves London. But she loves you too. And she knows that if she wants to be with you in the long term, she'll probably have to leave London. Maybe even leave her job. And that's a tough choice. She's struggling with it. Just like we all struggle when we have to choose between things we love. I think the problem with you two is that you don't really talk enough about the things that matter most to you. You're the strong, silent type. Ivy's a live wire. That doesn't mean you can't be very happy together. You really need to sort it out. And what I really need is more coffee.' Gabriel slapped him on the arm and went off to find some.

Was Gabriel right? Did Ivy still love him? Had he been completely wrong about Ivy and Jamie? He paced up and down until someone stopped in front of him. It was Laurel and she held out another plastic cup.

'Coffee?'

'Thanks. Gabriel's just gone looking for some.'

'I know. I saw him. How are you?'

'Confused. What were we talking about when Ivy… When the accident happened? I can't seem to remember much before seeing Ivy squashed between the seat and airbag.'

'I was telling you that I've been in love with you for probably my entire life.'

'Oh shit, Laurel. Are you… Are you serious?'

She smiled. 'I thought I was. And for a moment last night, I thought you might love me.'

'Oh Laurel. I do love you. But as—'

'It's okay, Ned. You love me as a friend. I know that. And I hope you always will. Because I'll always love you that way too. It's funny how, when love is unrequited, it takes on a magnitude it wouldn't have if that love was returned. I think loving you became a habit. I was addicted to being in love with you.'

'But now you're not?'

'Apparently not. My love for you is clearly shallow. I didn't know it until today. Until I talked to Kev the Rev. Although I didn't really know it then. It wasn't until about seven o'clock tonight that I suddenly realised I was in love with Jamie. I am in love with Jamie. For all the good that'll do me. It seems I go from one unrequited love to another.'

'Jamie? You're in love with Jamie?'

Laurel nodded and pulled a face. 'Great, isn't it? I certainly know how to pick them.'

'How does Jamie feel about you? Your love may not be unrequited this time. I mean…'

Laurel smiled. 'It's okay, Ned. I know what you mean. But Jamie's shown exactly what he thinks of me. Holly's just told me that he left this afternoon. Apparently, he got a call from his agent. They want him back already. Holly didn't know the details, other than it seems Mrs Finer holds more sway than her husband. And Mrs Finer wants Jamie in the next film.'

'So that's it? He's gone?'

'He's gone. May I give you some advice, Ned?'

'Yes.'

'Don't let Ivy go. I know things weren't perfect. And I know there'll be problems. But at the dance you asked me if I thought it was enough to love someone, and I said it was, if you loved them enough. I think if you truly love someone you can scale mountains together. You can capture the moon. You truly love Ivy, Ned. And from what Holly says, Ivy truly loves you. I think that's more than enough. And I think you need to go and tell her.'

'Thank you, Laurel. I'll do that. I'll do that right now. Jamie has no idea how lucky he could have been.' Ned kissed her on the cheek and went to find Ivy's cubicle.

Janet was sitting beside Ivy, holding her hand. She turned as Ned walked in.

'How is she?'

'Ned?' Ivy's eyes shot open although clearly with some effort. 'I'm fine. Thank you for what you did for me at the car.'

'I didn't do anything but I've come to tell you something.'

'Do you want me to leave?' Janet asked.

Ned shook his head. 'No. There's no need. Ivy Gilroy, I love you. I love you with all my heart and all my soul. And I don't care how different we are. And I don't care if we don't have many things in common. We can enjoy each other's differences. We can find things we both like. Please forgive me for behaving like an idiot. I thought you were in love with Jamie. I thought you wanted to be with him. I thought you wanted that whole celebrity lifestyle and I can't give you that. But I don't need to give you that. Your job gives you that. I may not like London and I may love Hideaway Down, but I love you more. And I want to be with you, wherever that is. Can we start again? But from now on, can we tell each other what we really want? Discuss things properly and find a way to work this out. Because tonight, for a moment there, I thought I might lose you, and *that* I just couldn't bear.'

Ivy nodded. 'Yes Ned. Yes please. And I've thought about it too, even more since I've been lying here and I don't care about celebrities, or London, or even my job anywhere near as much as I love you. I was frightened. Frightened of how much I love you. Terrified of what that means. Because what it means is I would give up everything to be with you.'

Janet sniffed, wiped her eyes and got to her feet. 'Oh dear God, will you come over here Ned Stelling? I'm going to get some coffee and then I'm coming back. So you've got ten minutes to kiss and make up.'

Ned beamed at her. He would make good use of every second.

Chapter Twenty-Nine

Laurel read the text from Graydon and smiled. Her brother had got a new girlfriend and a photo was attached. Graydon looked happy and so did the girlfriend who had the same blonde hair and similar angelic features. That should please their mother.

The café door opened and Laurel glanced up, slipping her phone beneath the counter as she did so.

'What can I get you? Oh! It's you.'

'A better menu,' Jamie said. 'I see nothing's changed in a month.'

Laurel couldn't believe her eyes. What was he doing back here? Neither Holly nor Gabriel had told her he was coming. He looked different. Gone was the pale complexion; instead his face was lightly tanned. His hair was as black as she remembered and it shimmered in the sunlight filtering through the window where he stood. The leather jacket was the same but his jeans were faded blue and his light blue V-neck T-shirt enhanced the tan on his neck.

'You're wrong, as usual. Some things *have* changed in a month. Holly's bookshop is ready to open and Petunia and Bartram are engaged.'

'And you, Laurel. There's something different about you.'

'There's a bit less of me. I've lost some weight. And you've gained some colour. They've let you out of the coffin, have they?'

'I've been using the boots I bought that day in

Eastbourne. It turns out that I quite like walking. Who knew? Things didn't work out with you and Ned then? I'm sorry about that.'

Laurel shrugged. 'We don't always get what we want.'

'Don't we? It seems Ivy and Ned have.'

'Yes. Sorry. You should've asked her out whilst you had the chance.'

'I decided I didn't want to. You know me. I'm shallow like that.'

'Punched any studio bosses lately?'

'I haven't had the time. Or the inclination. I hear there's a dance at the church hall tonight. Are you going with anyone?'

Laurel grinned. 'We'll all be going. We always do. Everyone in the village goes.'

Jamie coughed. 'So I'm told. But are you going *with* anyone?'

'As in, 'a date' you mean?'

'Yes.'

'No. And I think we've had this conversation before. About a month ago.'

'Twenty-nine days ago, to be exact. But who's counting? Will you go with me?'

Laurel giggled. 'Are you asking me on a date?'

'Would you say yes if I were?'

'No.' She giggled louder.

'Then I'm not. What time do you finish here?'

'I close at six.'

'Great. I'll pick you up at seven-thirty and we'll have dinner in the pub.'

'Jamie! I'm not going on a date with you.'

'Of course you're not.'

'I'm serious.'

He tipped his head to one side. 'I don't remember that

bit last time.'

'That's because I didn't say it last time. And perhaps I should have. I am not going on a date with you.'

'Not even a non-date? Why not?'

'Well, for one thing, you live in Hollywood. And I'm not into one-night stands.'

'Who said anything about one night?'

'That's how long you stayed last time. Seriously, Jamie. What's the point?'

'The point is, Laurel French, I like you.'

'That's nice. But I'm still not going on a date with a movie star from Hollywood.'

'Fair enough.' Without another word, he turned around and walked away.

Had that actually just happened? Or had it been some bizarre daydream? One minute she was looking at a photo of Graydon and his girlfriend, the next looking up into the deep, coffee coloured eyes of the man she loved. A man she had missed more than she had thought possible after knowing him for only one day, but a man she had missed with all her heart since he had got on a plane twenty-eight days ago without as much as a goodbye. She had told herself she must forget him. Having one long-term unrequited love was bad enough. Having two, was certifiable madness. She had got over Ned completely. She would get over Jamie, too.

The door opened again and Jamie came back in. Without a word, he strode towards her. Her heart pounded against her chest as he covered the distance between them and then, like a hero in a romance novel, he leapt over the counter and pulled her to him in a passionate kiss.

'Oh my God!' Laurel said, trying to regain her composure when he finally eased his hold on her. 'For years I've imagined someone doing that, I never dreamt it would be you.'

He smiled. 'Well the thing is, Laurel French, it seems I'm having trouble getting you out of my head. Every coffee shop I go to I'm looking for a *Laurel* but it's never on the menu.'

'So you're telling me you've come all this way just for a cup of coffee.'

'And a kiss. And to take you to the dance.'

'And then you'll get back on a plane to the bright lights of Hollywood.'

'No. *We'll* get on a plane to the bright lights of Hollywood. I've arranged it all with Trixie, with a little help from Holly and Gabriel.'

'What? I can't go to Hollywood. I've got a business to run.'

'It's only for two weeks. Then I'll have finished the first lot of filming, and we can come back here.'

'Come back here? What are you saying? That you're going to stay here a while?'

'A long while, if things go to plan. I mentioned that perhaps my character, Adam should spend a year or two in England. Mrs Finer thinks so too. We'll start filming sometime in the autumn. Until then I've got the summer off.'

'You're very sure of yourself, aren't you?'

'I'm very sure of two things.'

'Oh? What?'

'I'm very sure that I'm in love with you. And I'm very sure that it will last a lifetime.' He pulled her closer. 'And as I'm a vampire, that means you're stuck with me for eternity.'

'Damn. I suppose that means I've got to get a better menu.'

Jamie laughed. 'Well, that must mean you love me too.

And that also means I've got a date for the dance tonight.'

'That means you've got a date for any dance on any night. And yes, Jamie McDay, I love you too. Oh! And as this will officially be our first date, I've got a new first date rule.'

'Since when?'

'Since you kissed me.'

He grinned at her and something in his dark eyes twinkled. 'Okay. What's the new rule?'

'That we have to have sex on our first date.'

'Now that's a rule I like.'

And he proved how much he liked it when he kissed her again.

***

THE END

Thank you

Thank you so much for reading, *Catch A Falling Star*. I hope you enjoyed it and if so, please consider telling your friends and/or posting a short review. Word of mouth is an author's best friend and very much appreciated.

COMING SOON

Walking on Sunshine
A Hideaway Down Novel (Book 3)

You simply need to take that step

Lucy Draycourt doesn't like taking time out from her busy life as a litigation lawyer but her friend, Beatrix Welsley says Lucy needs to 'find herself'... so they're going to Beatrix's, Aunt Petunia's wedding. Lucy can't see how this will help – and besides, she doesn't need to find herself. Just because she was given away at birth doesn't mean she's 'lost'. Who cares that she was adopted? Her childhood was perfect so it doesn't bother her. Or does it? Is her endless search for recognition really a search for something else? And what makes Beatrix think Lucy will find it at Petunia Welsley's wedding?

Evan Foster needs a break. He's done nothing but work for several years and his life is, frankly, a mess. This week his uncle Bartram's getting married and it's been a while since Evan's seen him. Perhaps this wedding's come at just the right time. Or maybe not. This week, two years ago, Evan's fiancée ran off with his business partner and it's now abundantly clear that they're not coming back. He needs to make plans for the future, but it's difficult to move forward when you're still living in the past.

But as Petunia Welsley, the bride-to-be would say: 'You can't see the sun if you're staring into clouds, but sometimes all you need to do is to take a step in a different direction and you'll be walking on sunshine.'

To see details of my other books, please go to the books page on my website or scan the QR code, below.
http://www.emilyharvale.com/books.

***

Scan or tap the code above to see Emily's books on Amazon

To read about me, my books, my work in progress and competitions, freebies, or to contact me, pop over to my website http://www.emilyharvale.com. To be the first to hear about new releases and other news, you can subscribe to my Readers' Club newsletter via the 'Sign me up' box. Or why not come and say 'Hello' on Facebook, Twitter, Instagram or Pinterest. Hope to chat with you soon.

Printed in Great Britain
by Amazon